THREADS of HOME

THREADS of HOME
A Quilting Story
Part 2

JODI BARROWS

MOODY PUBLISHERS

CHICAGO

© 2014 by
JODI BARROWS

Edited by Pam Pugh
Interior design: Ragont Design
Cover design: LeVan Fisher Design
Cover photos: © pixelworks studios, shutterstock/wimclaes/
V. J. Matthew/milyana
Author photo: Holly Paulson: Sillyheads Photography

Library of Congress Cataloging-in-Publication Data

Barrows, Jodi.
    Threads of home / Jodi Barrows.
        pages cm. — (A Quilting story ; Part 2)
    Summary: "The past threatens to destroy the good days ahead. Liz has overcome the emptiness of her husband's death, the hardships of the trip west and even the robbery and murder of her beloved grandfather. Standing at the altar, she feels hope for the first time in many years. Settling into their new home in Fort Worth, Texas, the cousins begin to build a new life now that Grandfather is gone, but their minds are never at rest. Abby initiates the work necessary to start a new school while Liz works in the mercantile. Emma stands firm as a herd of cattle and cowboys come dangerously close, sparking a new venture for Emma—she learns that providing the cowboys with food and shelter, for both them and their horses, can bring extra income into the household. But Emma can't do it alone; she enlists the help of the lighthearted Megan. As the women gather at the quilting frame, relationships grow strong as women work together while facing the hardships and joys of a life on the prairies of Texas. As the four cousins forge a new family amid the unfamiliar ways of those living on the plains, feel the suffering of loss and the joy of true love found."—Provided by publisher.
        ISBN 978-0-8024-0938-6 (pbk.)
    1. Domestic fiction. I. Title.
PS3602.A83735T59 2013
813'.6—dc23

                                          2013027770

We hope you enjoy this book from River North Fiction by Moody Publishers. Our goal is to provide high-quality, thought-provoking books and products that connect truth to your real needs and challenges. For more information on other books and products written and produced from a biblical perspective, go to www.moodypublishers.com or write to:

River North Fiction
Imprint of Moody Publishers
820 N. LaSalle Boulevard
Chicago, IL 60610

1 3 5 7 9 10 8 6 4 2

Printed in the United States of America

Fort Worth, Texas
August–December 1856

Today wasn't her first time as a bride, so she shouldn't be nervous. But this time was different. There in front of her was a church filled with people and Thomas was lovingly waiting for her at the altar.

Liz Bromont's long blonde hair fell loosely over her shoulders and her brilliant blue eyes sparkled with excitement as she peeked out to see the front of the church. She ran her fingers down the silky smooth fabric of her borrowed wedding dress, relishing the overlay of lace and seed pearls sewn across the bodice as well as the pleated insert on the center of the skirt. The shoulders of the dress rested perfectly across the tips of Liz's porcelain shoulders, her skin smooth and creamy next to the princess cut neckline. She wasn't accustomed to being arrayed in this style or having so many curls in her hair.

"I'd never be able to get any work done in this dress," Liz said softly as she twisted her shoulders in the elegant white gown and settled her hands on her slim waist.

With continued appreciation, Liz thought about the friends and family who had come to celebrate the union. This little, deserted fort had welcomed them and supported them in the death of her grandfather and now in her marriage. She had intended to have a simple wedding, but once her family and friends got involved, it started to grow. When her sister, Megan, had asked, "What will you wear?" her friend Anna had offered her own wedding dress, which had begun her own life of marital happiness. Megan went to work with her sewing skills, until the dress fit Liz perfectly.

Then Mrs. Perkins said she would arrange a dinner to follow the ceremony. She asked Zeke Goodwin and his friend Smithy to play lively dancing music. She spread the word in the community and before Liz knew it, the simple wedding was turning into a full-grown party.

When Liz protested the large gathering, her cousin Abby said, "And what better reason to celebrate?" making it a done deal.

Everyone, herself included, needed a celebration to put them back where they needed to be after the murder of Lucas. Liz thought about what she had told herself and others over and over again: A person can sit in the sadness of the past and allow it to ruin the future or else choose to move forward with life. Liz wouldn't allow the past to destroy the good days ahead. She would push through the emptiness of her first husband's death, the hardships of the trip west, and even the terrifying robbery at gunpoint of the mercantile that had ended with the murder of her beloved grandfather Lucas Mailly.

Liz's mother was the daughter of Lucas and Claire Mailly. But when both their parents had died in a fire, she and Megan had come to live at the Mailly timber mill in Louisiana. The girls were cherished and loved and raised to be strong, intelligent Southern women. Liz would always be a Mailly at heart, even though she didn't carry the name.

And she was happy, truly happy, about the marriage. It wasn't just for convenience. She had developed feelings for this man. Thomas had been a friend of the family for years; in fact, he had been a close friend of her late husband and the foreman for her late grandfather's timber mill. He had a patient persistence and had finally won her heart over with his love and kindness.

How could Liz tell her friends and family no to a boot-stompin' Texas wedding party?

She treasured each and every one of them and vowed to herself that she would in turn be there for them when they needed her.

Abby and Emma, their Mississippi cousins, had traveled with her and Megan in the wagon train to Texas. Abby was the new schoolteacher, and Emma, well, Emma wasn't sure what she would do next.

She was the youngest of the Mailly granddaughters and struggled with finding her place in the world. Emma had tried to get along with her heavy-handed father, but was rebuffed or ignored at every turn. Now, having been held too tightly, she was growing rebellious, and seemed to buck against everyone and everything. Liz so wanted Emma to find her way that she encouraged her every chance she could. Emma had a hard time trusting that anyone, even Liz, might have her best interest at heart.

Liz watched Abby pull an embroidered hankie from her bag and dab at her eyes as she waited for the ceremony to unfold before her. Emma sniffled too, and accepted a handkerchief from her sister, Abby.

Sitting on another bench were the three Texas Rangers the girls had befriended on their journey west. Grandpa Lucas had hired the men to escort the four women to the Texas town as well as the wagonload of gold acquired from the sale of the timber mill. Despite encountering some perils and getting lost for a time, the group had made it safely to Fort Worth.

Tex was the old weathered captain of the Rangers who had appointed himself as guardian over the four young women following the tragic death of their grandfather. Liz suspected that he felt somewhat responsible since he was away at the time of the robbery and hadn't been able to capture the known bandits beforehand.

Near Tex were Jackson and Colt, dressed up in their Sunday best; they were the other two Rangers the family had developed a close friendship with. It was good to have them in town for a while, especially since the ongoing trouble with the neighboring community of Birdville.

Anna, the pastor's wife and her friend, stood with Liz at the back of the church.

"You look beautiful. Now be still or you will tumble out of that dress," she teased, tucking a straying blonde strand of hair back in place. "Are you ready?" Anna moved aside to let Liz through.

Liz bit the side of her lip and nodded her head. "One foot in front of the other," she told herself as she stepped closer to the back of the aisle. Anna smiled at her and provided her the go-ahead by offering her a small push. Liz took the arm her twelve-year-old son Luke offered, and together they made their way up the aisle toward Thomas.

Her groom was wearing a crisp, white button-down shirt with a black string tie at the collar. He was strong and handsome, but what she had come to love was the inner strength of this man. She realized, as she locked eyes with his, that this wonderful man made her heart skip a beat.

Thomas looked natural and at ease, except for twisting the small, sterling silver wedding band at the tip of his little finger. Liz smiled as she watched him, remembering that this was the ring he had bought months ago when the peddler Skelly came to town.

Thomas swallowed hard, causing his Adam's apple to move up and down as he watched his bride float toward him. Liz had finally agreed to marry him. He had dreamed for years of this day and couldn't be more excited. To come home to her each night was what he had always longed for. She was a force to be reckoned with, but he had loved her for years.

Liz saw her sister waiting at the front of the church in her beautiful blue dress, eyes glistening. The two were inseparable and loved each other dearly. They sounded alike when they talked and often finished each other's sentences. They both knew there would be tears today and tried to avoid each other's eyes—tears of joy as Liz and Thomas were united in marriage, and tears for missing their grandfather.

Luke kissed his mother and took his place beside Thomas, a nervous smile pasted on his face as he waited for the two to tie the knot. Liz's heart started to ache as she thought of what young Luke had endured. It was hard enough for her as an adult to have endured the sudden loss of Caleb, her husband and Luke's father, and now Grandpa Lucas, let alone a child to take it all in. But Liz knew her son was fond of Thomas and hoped he would soon love him like a father.

Thomas took Liz's small hand as they turned to face Pastor Parker. The words of the ceremony spoke of love, patience, and forgiveness. Liz lingered on his words, knowing how quickly a loved one can be lost. When Thomas finished slipping the band on Liz's finger, the clergyman introduced them to the congregation as Mr. and Mrs. Thomas Bratcher. Thomas grinned from ear to ear and swept his bride up in a kiss. The couple went down the aisle hand in hand and greeted their guests as they congratulated the newlyweds and then headed for the feast and dancing outside.

Thomas and Liz finally exited the church. Thomas looked down at his beautiful bride, overjoyed to see that the happiness on her face mirrored his own. Her glowing smile delighted him. Studying her, he said, "You look beautiful, Mrs. Bratcher," and brushed his lips with hers.

Mrs. Perkins had outdone herself, and a delicious meal was laid out for all to enjoy. Liz hadn't eaten much during the hectic day and she was hungry. The smell of food was enticing. "Thomas," she exclaimed, with her hand covering her stomach. "I'm famished. I could eat a whole chicken." She smiled and led him toward the tables of food. Thomas laughed as his stride matched hers and she went to fill her plate. He smiled inwardly at his strong-willed lady and suspected this wouldn't be the last time she'd take his hand and pull him along.

※　※　※

When the meal was over, Zeke and Smithy began their music while couples headed to the makeshift dance floor. Thomas pulled his bride in that direction. He wanted to hold her close, drift with the music, and soak it all in.

Jackson was the tallest man in the crowded room and could easily look over everyone's heads to find Megan. He had gotten to know the petite and feisty young woman with brown silky hair on the wagon train as they traveled to Fort Worth. She was funny, easy to talk to, and just loved life. She saw every detail, even the smallest ones, and took enjoyment in them, looking for the best in everything. He found himself wanting to be around her often. He quickly grabbed her as the music got louder and livelier. She smiled and took his hand.

"You look lovely in your blue dress," Jackson said, smiling at her, knowing all the work she had put into it. She placed her hand on his broad shoulder as he danced her onto the wooden planks among the other couples whirling about.

Colt stuck a finger into the collar of his shirt and ran it around his neck to loosen his string tie as he looked around the gathering. After spotting Emma watching the action alone, he mustered the courage to ask the young woman to dance.

"Let's dance," he whispered in her ear, and was rewarded with a smile. She willingly took his hand as he spun her off in a circle just as the musicians began another tune.

Luke watched the dancing as he finished pulling the last bit of meat from the chicken bone. Wiping his fingers on the inside of his pants leg he found a group of youngsters trying to pluck up the nerve to get out on the dance floor. Luke confidently smiled at his buddies and led the way, inviting a surprised young lady into the midst of the music.

With the deep blue haze of evening settling in and the fireflies magically lighting the edge of the woods, Zeke and Smithy tapped the soles of their well-worn boots to the beat of the Virginia reel. Zeke stroked the strings of his fiddle while Smithy ran his hands and mouth skillfully across his harmonica. Couples faced each other in a line and changed their pattern of steps for the foot stomping dance. The floor began to vibrate and hum with the pounding feet, adding to the merriment of the evening.

When Thomas and Liz bowed to each other for the beginning of the dance, he whispered words of love just for her ear. Her cheeks turned pink as she laughed and stepped backwards, extending her arms in the dance pattern of the Virginia reel.

The couples swayed to the music, locking elbows and trading partners as they skipped. The women's cotton dresses, a rainbow of colors and styles, billowed out with each swirl of their feet. This was nothing like the galas in the South, Liz thought, remembering ruffled, hooped skirts floating across perfectly shined marble floors. She already understood that here in Texas, a woman's beauty wasn't in what she wore but in what grew from within. Here her heart and soul were woven tightly together by the love of her husband, the smiles of her children, and the appreciation of the land she lived on. It was a simple beauty which could drop a grown man to his knees.

Thomas leaned on a post and rested a moment as a group of chatty ladies whisked his wife away. His eyes were drawn to the old Ranger, Tex, who appeared to be deep in thought and leaning on a post of his own. Tex didn't look at Thomas when he spoke. He only adjusted the brim of his hat, expressing his thoughts as he did so.

"Things changing, you know. With each day, they are changing."

Thomas glanced at the dancing couples and looked at the Mailly women clustered with several other laughing females. As he considered Tex's words, he thought about this wild sprawling country called Texas, where friendships were kindled and not misused, where love was real and not the merging of two family empires, and where trust was an honest thing a person could hold and treasure. He was sure this Mailly family's coming to town had changed Tex too. They accepted him, knowing without spoken words that he had bruised and broken places within. They made him stronger and gave him the desire to be a better man.

Taking the time to care and trust was a rare luxury in Tex's business, Thomas knew, but these women beckoned it.

"Lucas should be here," Tex said, not for the first time. "He should be the one watching his family celebrate a wedding, not an old, used-up man like me."

CHAPTER 2

S amuel Smith was a lawyer who favored the wide open countryside over four walls of a law office or courtroom. Not that he didn't like the law or politics; it just usually involved stuffy buildings and sometimes stuffy people, often men who were egotistic. He preferred the back of his horse and the view it provided.

Now that he was a self-appointed city elder for the up-and-coming town of Fort Worth, his work involved, among other things, getting the school going in their community and writing contracts for land deeds of the homesteaders.

Just by living on the land for three years and making improvements, a homesteader could acquire ownership of the property, but the arrangement was under Texas law rather than that of the U.S. government. The state was unique among others in the union in that it had been an independent country: the Republic of Texas. When it had been annexed in 1845, the agreement was that Texas would retain rights to all vacant or unappropriated land within its borders.

According to the homestead law Samuel was working with, a settler could pay a filing fee of twelve dollars to a traveling land agent and take residence of the land immediately. Or he could travel to Austin himself, which was often a great distance, and file a land deed in person.

Either way held risks. A land agent might not return, due to any number of factors. Travel was slow and could be perilous, and north

Texans were often reluctant both to chance a journey and to leave their land unattended. To help with the problem, an agent was situated in Medlin, a settlement along the north branch of the Trinity River. Samuel's role was to set up paperwork, file documents, secure finances— all of which helped the homesteaders with legalities as well as peace of mind as they began working on their 160 acres.

Samuel was also involved with settling the county record dispute with Birdville.

Birdville. The town selected a few years before as Tarrant County's first county seat and the other side of an ongoing dispute with Fort Worth, which aspired to the distinction. A second, special election had been held recently, giving the edge to Fort Worth, and giving rise to rumors of men voting who didn't live in the county and other dubious suspicions. The county records had to be carefully kept safe and secure from those who sought to steal them.

As he wrote contracts for the land deeds, Samuel reflected that it seemed like Texas was giving its land away and settlers were quick to start homesteading procedures, especially now that most of the Indian wars were pushed farther west.

Samuel's father, suitably dubbed Smithy by the cavalry, was the blacksmith for the fort. He and his wife had followed the troops west as they pushed to civilize the new frontier.

Anna Parker, his sister, had married the army preacher. Pastor Heath Parker, with his well-worn Bible and knowledge of how to live a good life, preached in a way that everyone could understand. He made a man want to live according to what God wanted rather than invoking a fear of hell and brimstone the way most preachers he'd heard did. And Samuel had never seen a man love a woman like Parker loved Anna.

Smithy, the Parkers, and Samuel decided to stay in Fort Worth after the army moved on. By the time Lucas Mailly and his four granddaughters arrived, the small community was growing and expanding along the Trinity River. Ranches popped up and farmland was planted with cotton and other crops. The present and future looked promising, and Samuel enjoyed being on the ground floor, growing it up right.

Samuel, Smithy, and Parker had written letters for months seeking a teacher for their small community with not much luck until they mentioned it in a letter to Lucas Mailly. He told them one of his granddaughters was a teacher and was coming with them when they moved to Texas. The Fort Worth leaders offered her the position and she accepted. This was a perfect match and they were very proud of the teacher they got with Miss Abigail Wilkes. She was the prim and proper type, used to the long list of "must-dos and must-nots" that teachers back east endured. She was a little jittery over the easygoing style of the West, where letter-of-the-law rules were overridden by necessity and survival. Samuel got a kick out of watching Abby being taken aback at the informality of the West. He knew she would settle in to the new bridle soon enough.

Samuel kicked his covers off as he deliberated about these things and considered the day ahead. It was time to quit lollygagging around and focus on his responsibilities. He had planned on riding out to his ranch land to do a little planning while the weather was still pleasant. However, ever since the Bratchers' wedding, he couldn't get Miss Abigail Wilkes off his mind. Yes, she was his responsibility, but this feeling of being intrigued with her was more than a business matter and it bothered him.

He thought he would be much further along with building his ranch by now. But then the Mailly family had arrived in town and things began to happen. Now that the wedding was over, maybe he could get the school settled and get on with his own business.

"Yup, that's what I need," he told himself. "Some fresh air to clear my mind and think."

After getting dressed, he walked to the stables to get his horse saddled. He barely spoke to his dad, except to say, "Can you saddle a horse for the schoolteacher?"

Smithy looked at his son and held his tongue, only commenting, "Sure thing, Samuel."

Early on, Thomas Bratcher had discovered a Texas grant for education. The state would give money to a school if it could enroll at least twelve students. Abby had been delighted with the news and had been searching the farms and ranches for students of age.

Abby needed to convince the parents that an education was worth the effort and encourage the students to make the walk each day. However, she didn't know the outlying area yet and required help to find the families; besides, it was too dangerous for her to be out by herself, so Samuel appointed himself as overseer of the schoolmarm from Mississippi. Mostly he ruffled her feathers and enjoyed watching her flutter around. She in turn made him promise to mind his manners and reluctantly let him accompany her to the outlying farms and ranches.

Samuel walked his horse from the stables to the Mailly home behind the mercantile. He saw Abby at the porch railing. How beautiful she looked, he noticed with pleasure. Her hair was pinned loosely and hung around her shoulders, not worn pulled tight to the back of her head like the fusty teachers he remembered from his boyhood. The morning breeze blew a wisp of her curly dark hair over her brown eyes. He was so intent on watching how they sparkled in the early sun hoping the slight smile that crossed her lips might be directed at him that he didn't even notice the newlyweds on the porch with her.

"Good morning." She greeted him as she pushed the stray hair away from her face.

"Good morning," he replied and then decided to get down to business. "We have a few kids to get enrolled in your classroom. They live a ways out and I'm here to take you to meet them."

Abby turned to face him square on, wondering at his assumption that she would go with him.

"Abby, I'm responsible for our school, which includes you and the students. I'm here to assist you." He watched her and twisted his hat in his hands.

Abby couldn't tell if he was teasing or not. Back in Mississippi it wouldn't be proper to ride out alone with a man, much less a single man, but she was going to have to get used to Texas ways. She did need help, and no one else was available to spend time escorting her across the countryside.

"Will it take most of the day to visit the remaining families?" she asked.

Samuel couldn't help feeling like a child standing before a teacher after being caught in a mischievous prank. "Could," he said, most mannerly, wanting her to say yes and trying to hurry her along.

Abby paused, thinking it over. "I can pack a basket lunch and maybe we can get all of the families visited today," she mused. "I only have a few more families to visit and then I'll have the required twelve children." She disappeared into the house to pack the lunches.

Thomas and Liz had been watching the exchange from their rocking chairs on their porch, until Liz left to help Abby with the food. Thomas stepped up, smiling. He was happy to see Samuel had his eye on someone other than his Liz. When they had first come to the settlement, Thomas thought he would have to smack Samuel a time or two. But for weeks now he had suspected the lawyer had his eyes on Abby. And Thomas was glad. After all, Samuel was a neighboring landowner, and in this raw territory a man needed as many friends as he could get.

Samuel patted his horse and tossed the reins over the post rail as Thomas came down the porch steps. Samuel swiped at some trail dust on his sleeve and noticed the amused look on Thomas's face.

"What?" Samuel asked.

"You tell me," Thomas threw back, jokingly. "You got something under your saddle? You sure were in deep thought as you walked over here."

Samuel used his arm to wipe beads of sweat from his brow then fitted his hat back on his head. "Got a lot on my mind is all. Tossed all night."

Thomas smiled to himself. He had suspected Samuel was sweet on Abby weeks ago. But with the robbery and murder and the trouble with the county records, and then the wedding celebration, everyone had plenty of other things on their minds.

"When are you heading out to your land?" Thomas changed the topic.

"Just as soon as I can get those kids in school. I need some fresh air," Samuel replied, looking forward to some thinking time.

"Well, we're neighbors now, you know. If you want to ride together, I've been thinking of looking my place over. I'm anxious to get to work."

Liz and Abby appeared again with a basket of goodies covered in a red-checkered cloth.

Samuel pulled the reins from the post and turned his horse to leave. "Abby, let me carry the basket and we'll walk over to the stable for your horse. Smithy should have it saddled and ready." He glanced to Abby's new riding skirt. It was a nice one, probably like well-to-do women would wear on a Southern plantation.

"Liz, thank you for the lunch," Abby said as her boots clicked on each step. She passed the basket to Samuel and started to pull on her gloves.

It dawned on Samuel that she had already planned on going riding that day. With or without him he wasn't so sure.

"Oh, and Thomas," she turned her head, "thank you again for your help on the grant. It would have taken me so long to get funds from back east. I know we can get the remaining supplies on the next freight wagon."

Thomas nodded as he felt Liz put her hand inside his. Standing by his side, Liz watched her cousin and the handsome lawyer walk away.

Lucas would be proud, she thought. They were all healing.

CHAPTER 3

It was still dark in north Texas when Abby buttoned her sage green cotton dress. She quietly shut her bedroom door, as she didn't want to wake her younger sister. Both sisters normally rose at the same time each morning, but today Abby was getting up especially early. She had a busy day planned and she needed every minute.

She still had forty-five minutes before the sun rose and the local rooster would start his morning announcement. She found the lamp in the darkness of the kitchen and struck a match to light it. A warm glow soon surrounded her as she looked around the spacious kitchen. She was grateful for her living accommodations, as some teaching assignments only came with small sleeping quarters. God had been good to Abby in both of her previous teaching positions and she was thankful for them.

This home was far smaller than the one she had grown up in, but the rooms were surprisingly spacious. The house they found when they arrived in Fort Worth had been the captain's home at the fort and he had it built with many luxuries, as he wanted to keep his wife happy for as long as possible. But in the end, she couldn't stick out the rough life and went back to her parents in Boston.

Abby and Emma's parents still lived in the white-pillared plantation home where the girls had been born. Abby had never intended to disappoint her parents, but she knew they didn't understand her love for teaching or why she craved her independence. They didn't mind so much when she went away to achieve a higher education. Her father had banked on the thought that she would meet a man of importance and change her way of thinking. Several men did take notice of the witty young woman with high cheekbones and an unquenchable search for knowledge, but no man could hold her attention for long. Abby loved learning and spent her time gaining as much schooling as she could.

When her education was complete, she returned home to Mississippi not far from her family home. Once again, her parents thought she would teach a year, not more than two, and then settle down as the wife of one of the many local businessmen who so eagerly sought her attention. But Abby was devoted to educating her students and spent her hours in the evening reading about new things to teach them.

Since Abby appeared to have exactly what she had worked for, it came as a complete surprise to all of the community when she announced she was leaving her position at the end of the school year and going west to start a frontier school at a deserted fort in Texas.

Her mother nearly became sick with worry upon this news and tried unsuccessfully to change her daughter's mind. Finally, Abby promised that she wouldn't sign a contract with her new position until she arrived in Texas and was certain that this was what she desired. Abby's mother did find comfort in the fact that she would be with her cousins and grandfather. If her mother had really known how alone they would be in their travels to Fort Worth, she would have been mortified.

Abby's father, John Wilkes, was a heavy-handed man who loved his family but was unprepared to raise two daughters. Neither girl behaved like other young women in the community. He had no idea that his father-in-law, Lucas, was the one to blame for the free-spirited women. Abby and Emma spent many summers at the Mailly home in Louisiana, enjoying time with their cousins and with Grandpa Lucas, keeping him company as he still missed Granny Claire. Lucas taught his granddaughters how to think and how to make their mark in the world. It made no difference to him that they were women.

So it just seemed right when the letter arrived asking if they wanted to go west. Lucas had been talking of this for years. It was only a matter of when, and the granddaughters knew this. Lucas made the arrangements for Abby to be hired as the teacher at the abandoned fort.

Lucas tried to convince his daughter and son-in-law to sell out and move with them before the upheaval to the country Lucas was certain would come. John dismissed him and his ridiculous predictions about an impending civil war and momentous change coming to their way of life. John Wilkes would never dream of selling out and leaving his home. What would he do in the West without his plantation and slaves to work it?

Abby found most men to be like her father, consumed by their work and staying ahead of their peers. The thoughts and feelings of "the wife" and daughters needn't be considered. Even as a young child Abby had realized that her father was disappointed that he had no sons.

The South was a part of Abby. She loved the rolling hills with enormous oak trees stretching out to shade the plantation, the moss hanging lazily from the branches, the sweet smell of magnolias floating on the humid breeze. She would lean against her favorite tree with her studies and listen to the songs that drifted up from the fields. She would always remember the plaintive spirituals that her father's slaves crooned as they worked.

Nellie was one of those slaves and the one Abby missed the most. She wasn't much older than she and Emma were and had been given to them when they were young girls. Even then Abby couldn't understand how another human being could be given as a gift. Abby and Emma loved Nellie and she them, and it was as though they had all grown up together. When they left Mississippi Nellie wanted to go with them, and they wanted her to come, but their father wouldn't allow it. Nellie was more heartbroken than their own mother was at their departure. Abby talked to her father, trying persistently to convince him to let Nellie go, but to no avail. Nellie swore she would find them someday. Abby wished she could get a letter off to Nellie but knew that even if she could get it there, no one would read it to her. Someday, she would try to get Nellie to their Texas home. Even though it seemed impossible, she would mention it to the others and see what they could do. Emma was so upset with her father about Nellie that she refused to bid him farewell.

Abby was sorry to leave while hard feelings remained, and tried in vain to mend things between Emma and their father. In the end, she held no sadness in her heart for her Mississippi home, only fond memories.

Now she gazed into the small mirror above the washstand close to the back door. As the lamp chased out the darkness, she could see her reflection. She was pretty, with shiny brown hair that had a mind of its own. The curl in her hair gave her otherwise prim-and-proper schoolteacher mien a softer edge. She tried to tame a stray curl she had missed in the darkness of her bedroom and smiled. How could any of her students take her seriously if she looked like the mythical monster Medusa?

Her expressive eyes could speak to students without her saying a word. Her countenance could rap a student as hard as any ruler could. Any child would sit straighter, write neater, try harder, and stop teasing when Abby gave "the look." Yet her sternness and discipline belied the tenderness she held for the children she taught, and she was quick to pass out encouragement. Even though her years of teaching could be counted with a few fingers, wisdom and knowledge were lodged sharply behind her chocolate brown eyes.

Abby had missed a button while dressing in the darkness of her room. Her neatly groomed fingers tried to work the button, but it fell off in her hand. She would just have to wait to sew it back on. The missing button was at her neck, so it would not pose a problem. She placed it in a small crock on the tabletop and went back to the mirror for one last look.

Abby was taller than her sister and the two cousins she had come to Fort Worth with, but not taller than most other women. As she studied herself in the mirror she saw a woman who could afford to gain a pound or two. Her mother would certainly be trying to fatten her up if she were present. Her hands smoothed the skirt of her cotton dress and one petticoat. Back home in Mississippi she could never get away with only wearing one. Some counties required teachers to wear as many as seven or eight petticoats. "Maybe that is why I look slimmer here," she thought. As she moved away from the mirror, she tried one last time to secure the curl that continually fell across her face. She had no time for primping today.

The wood stove was still warm. "Wonderful," she murmured as she stoked it to life and placed the already prepared coffeepot over the burner. She pushed the kindling into the open door of the stove's belly and flames leapt to greet it. Soon the coffee would be jumping in the enamel pot and Abby would be on her way. She had many things to do, and she was mentally putting the items on her list in order when she heard a scratch on the door as it creaked open.

A black bushy-haired dog blinked his eyes and sleepily came to sit by her feet. Bear was actually Luke's dog. When Luke was a toddler, he thought the puppy was a baby bear and the name stuck. Luke tried to teach him tricks, but the dog mostly wanted the treat. Abby reached down to rub the pet that obviously wasn't ready to be awakened.

"Good morning, Bear," she whispered, kneeling down, as her green skirt puddled around her gracefully.

Luke appeared in the doorway rumpled and fully dressed. His thick blond hair was still uncombed as he reached for his hat and boots, but his eyes were alert and shone with excitement.

"Did I wake you? I tried to be quiet," she told him.

"Hey, Miss Abby," he said matter-of-factly, "you didn't wake us. We're headed down to the bridge. Got a big fish to catch this morning." He now had his boots pulled on and his hat firmly planted on his head. "But don't worry none. I'll be back by late mornin' to paint your porch. I promise it will look right smart on your first day of school."

Abby loved this boy and looked, bemused, over his wrinkled state. Luke Bromont had a smile that brought life into the room on that pre-dawn morning. It was pleasing to see it on his youthful face.

Luke grinned again and said, "Yup, slept in my clothes, can't keep them boys waitin', or that big fish!"

Luke opened the door and slapped the side of his leg twice. The sleepy dog trotted out the open door with his master. Luke picked up the fishing pole that was leaning on the back porch and hustled toward the tree line hiding the river.

Abby watched Luke and his dog as they met up with another young man. In the dim light, Abby saw two broad-shouldered boys looking like men, with a purpose in their stride, when they walked. An odd foreboding came over her as she watched them, but she shook it off. Of course Luke and his friends would be careful fishing by the broken bridge. They weren't toddlers, after all, and Luke was a responsible boy.

As she watched them walk away, she suddenly gasped. "Oh my, Luke was looking me in the eye," she realized. "When did he grow so tall and filled out?" She wondered how the two growing boys—young men, really—would fit on her school benches!

As she stood in the doorway, she could hear horses from one street over, in front of the mercantile and down by Smithy's Livery.

She wondered if every early morning was typically busy as this one. The coffeepot was now hopping on the fire and a few transparent brown bubbles appeared at the spout. She shut the door and went to fill her cup. The pink gathered curtain fell into place over the glass as the door clicked shut and she walked away.

Just as Abby was gathering her things to leave, a small pink tint began to grace its color in the east and she heard a rooster crow. She banked the fire and pushed the hot coffee over to a cooler spot on the stove. She placed her list of responsibilities in her bag and put the cup of warm liquid to her lips. The smell of coffee was wonderful but she did enjoy her cup of tea more. But today began early and she knew she needed the jolt of a strong cup of coffee to get her going.

She was out the door and down the path to the main dirt road when the rooster gave its second wakeup call. As she approached the wooden sidewalk of the town, she noticed that horses and riders were already there. It was still mostly dark as she stopped to study her surroundings.

The old Texas Ranger stepped out of the darkness on the wooden sidewalk.

"Miss Abby, what are you doing out so early?" he drawled.

"I might ask you the same," she returned. "You startled me." Her hot coffee trickled over her fingers when she jumped.

"Sorry, ma'am. You got business out? Didn't know your learnin' started so early in the day." As a lawman, Tex thought that he was entitled to know everyone's business. He didn't expect to see the schoolteacher out with the sunrise.

"I have a lot of preparation to do." She changed hands with her cup and shook the hot coffee off her now pink fingers and wondered why she tried to walk with her cup.

Abby saw two other Rangers she knew, Jackson and Colt. They were coming across the street from the direction of her school at the church. Pastor Parker was also with them.

Jackson tipped his hat to the schoolmarm. His hat made him look even taller than he was. "Good morning." Then he was all business and looked to his weathered boss. "All secure, we'll just get this wagon and head on down to Smithy's now."

Abby was now more curious than ever about what was happening.

"Mr. Tex?" She never knew what to call him. "What is happening, and what is all secure?"

"All is well, ma'am. Just rangerin' is all. If you find yourself up this early on a regular manner, we might have to just put you on the payroll," he said with a chuckle.

Abby relaxed and smiled. She did like the old Ranger. There was just something about him that appealed to her. Now that her grandfather had been brutally taken from them, it felt especially good and comforting to have Tex around. "Thank you. I have plenty to keep me out of trouble with my present employment, but I do hope you will always be watching in the dark corners for me."

She smiled and bid him goodbye.

As Abby crossed the street, she saw the wagon headed toward the livery. Pastor Parker drove while Jackson led the three horses that the Rangers had ridden into town. Colt, the youngest of the Rangers, sat in the back of the wagon swinging his boots. He blew the schoolteacher a kiss.

"I wish they wouldn't tease me so," Abby said to herself as she felt a blush rushing to her cheeks. She gave a slight wave to Colt as he bumped away in the wagon.

CHAPTER 4

As Abby made her way up the wooden steps to the church that would serve as her classroom during the week, a slight chill in the air reminded her that fall would soon be coming and she would need to carry her shawl. The church door opened quietly and the morning light streaked into the building with its bouncing rays.

She looked around before entering the large cloakroom. Jackets, wet shoes, and other miscellaneous items would soon be stored there. Pegs were on the wall at different heights as well as two shelves that would hold the lunch pails. Ahead of her was the spacious crossing of the church. Benches were lined up and a simple wood podium stood at the front. She walked to the front and remembered her first Sunday at the church. The Parkers had a big white dog named Angel that acted like he was attending the service and knew just when to sit or stand. Abby smiled at the memory. She moved to the side of the aisles where a wide doorway led to her classroom.

Abby walked to the front of the room—really the back of the church—and stood at her small desk and chair. They were still in good condition even though they had been left behind by the cavalry. A new blackboard was attached to the wall. She turned to face her empty classroom, and imagined it filled with students. To her right were small benches where two or three smaller students could sit and to her left four longer benches were ready for the older students. Most of those seats would be empty when school started. The fall harvest would not be complete until October, and only then would the older boys be able to join her class. Abby understood that the field work was important to the livelihood of those families and indeed for the whole community. The older youth had to do their share of the labor before they would be allowed to attend school.

It wouldn't be long before she would lose those students entirely. She reminded herself of the importance of working with each child independently. She would have to give them as much schooling as time allowed as long as they were there.

The schoolteacher was content with all she saw as she sat down and took inventory of the classroom. She took out a single sheet of paper from her desk and started to write out her roll of students. The first row of small benches would hold two little ones: Daniel Longmont and his sister Lillie. Daniel wasn't really old enough to be in school, but he would sit in front if their mother, Katie, sent him along with his sisters. Lillie was so cute with her small baby voice and her blonde curls bobbing. She was a timid little one but so ready to learn and please her pretty teacher. Katie Longmont had been educated well as a child back east, and had already started the learning process with her own children. Abby admired Katie for the time she had put into her family. Life on the ranch was busy enough without teaching the ABCs.

Abby was pleased as she remembered each student and put them in their proper seating order. She had spent many hours visiting each child in their family environment, learning as much about them as she could. And she didn't want to waste time in the classroom with the things that she could learn in their homes.

She was just completing the seating chart when she heard voices and racket coming from the other side of the church wall. Abby walked over to the doorway that opened to the sanctuary. Pastor Parker and Samuel, with the help of Jackson, were clumsily unloading a large chest the size of a table. Finally Jackson, the giant of the three, simply picked up the thing and placed it at the front of the church, all in one lofty motion. Parker and Samuel just stood and watched as he maneuvered the massive piece of furniture all alone.

"Hello, Miss Abby," Pastor Parker greeted her. "How is the school sizing up? Are we ready for the first day?" Pastor Parker was always in a fine mood, as if the sun rose for him alone each day.

"Hello, gentlemen. It's coming along well." She acknowledged each one with a smile and walked closer to the group of men. Her curiosity was piqued by the early morning activity of this group. "You're certainly busy this morning." Abby had young men in her class before and knew when something was up. This group was much older, but nevertheless up to something. They smiled at Abby mysteriously.

Jackson appeared to be close to the age of thirty. He was six foot four and weighed two hundred and fifty pounds and most of that was his heart of gold. His straight-as-a-stitch hair was a sandy blond color and hung over to the side under his cowboy hat. Abby discovered that the depths of his dark navy blue eyes were worth staring at until she made herself look away. He had a lot of muscle and was strong as an ox. Jackson's smile was contagious and he seemed to tackle life with enjoyment. He had been a Texas Ranger and had ridden with the old captain, Tex, since he was a young buck. He protected his superior in more ways than the old man would ever know.

Jackson actually had a lot in common with his horse, Zeus. The horse was faithfully devoted to the Rangers and seemed to have the strength of ten animals. Jackson and Zeus both had a calming nature and it transferred to other living creatures. Years before, the horse had walked up to their campfire one night while they were camping in a canyon and attached himself to Jackson. He thought the black stallion was as close to a soul mate as he would ever get and didn't see the need for any other. Zeus was always there, one step ahead of the situation. He had pulled Jackson, as well as the others, out of more than one scrape.

"Yes," she continued, "I am very excited for the first day."

"That's good news," Samuel told her. "Don't we still have a family or two to visit? I can help you get there." His voice was eager. He had enjoyed their day of riding to some of the outlying families and especially remembered with pleasure their picnic on a blanket spread carefully over the grass. He had purposely suggested saving the last households for another time.

Abby was always a little on edge around Samuel. He was different than the other men she had met at school or in her social circle in Mississippi. It was hard to keep her proper schoolteacher role when he was in the conversation. He always managed to coax her out of her schoolmarm manners with his teasing and that twinkle in his eye. He brought out a side of her personality that she hadn't known was there, and his ability to do so made her a little uneasy. How could she be professional around his schoolboy teasing?

Samuel smiled as Abby fidgeted. He enjoyed teasing her. They all did.

"Thank you, Mr. Smith." Abby calmed herself by not answering him directly.

She turned away and placed her focus on the ornate chest. It really didn't look like the biblical ark. There were no winged angels in gold overlooking it. But it was very elaborate.

"Will you tell me about this?" she asked Pastor Parker.

The pastor looked it over again. "I just wanted a table at the front of the church for special occasions. I think it would be better to have the offering box there. It will also work well to hold the elements for the Lord's Supper."

Pastor Parker admired the handiwork of Samuel and his father, Smithy.

"It is mighty special," Jackson said as he dusted the specialty woodwork on the front and polished the brass handles where his fingerprints were. Two small doors were located on the back and one long drawer across the top. The drawer was almost hidden.

"I need to get the rest of this project finished and be on my way. Tex is expecting me to ride over with a report." Jackson was almost out the door when he stopped. "Where was Luke hightailin' it off to so early this morning?"

Abby walked to the door, which Jackson was blocking. Jackson stepped aside so that Abby could slide through. "I guess it's just in the nature of a Ranger to be inquisitive," Abby teased. Then she added, "Oh, I hope they are careful. Luke said that he was going with some of the other boys to the river bridge to do some swimming and fishing. I'm concerned over their safety. It sounds like a dangerous place."

"Don't worry over a bunch of boys. It's just an end-of-summer ritual," Samuel asserted. He was standing with Abby and Jackson. "If it makes you feel any better, I will go out later this afternoon and check it out."

"Thank you."

Samuel paused for a moment. "Let me know if you need a ride out to Peter Graham's." He caught her eyes with his. "You know, it's my job to help out with the school."

Abby shook her head. "If you were in my classroom, Mr. Smith, I would have a talk with your parents about your sassy behavior."

"You still can." Samuel smirked. "Here comes my father now."

⚹　⚹　⚹

That same morning, Liz pulled a few large barrels through the red doors of her mercantile, positioning the barrels under the new windowpanes she had recently purchased from the peddler Skelly. She placed a large, blooming potted plant on top of each barrel and looked with satisfaction at the colors of the flowers next to her windows.

Dusting her hands on her apron she looked down the main road and saw her cousin Abby sweeping the school steps.

Liz watched Abby work and smiled with contentment at the homey sight. It gave her strength to see her family begin to enjoy life again. It's true, she thought. We have to take hold of our feelings and happiness. We choose every day.

She pushed her long braid behind her back and waved across to Abby, who smiled and returned the gesture. Liz was humming as she walked back through the new double doors of the mercantile and looked around. All was now complete except the final coat of paint on the front porch. When Luke comes by to complete the task, Abby will be finished with her school plan, Liz reasoned. She expected him to be there any moment to paint Abby's freshly swept porch.

※ ※ ※

Abby stopped sweeping for a moment, rested her hands at the top of the broom handle, and surveyed her surroundings as she stood on the steps. The schoolyard was as much a part of the school experience as the curriculum and classroom were. Everyone in the community had worked hard to make Abby's desires and needs for the school a reality.

The schoolyard was now flat and free of any rocks, weeds, or debris. The prairie grass that covered it at this time of year was burned and tan from the summer months, with barely a hint of green showing. The fallen trees and leaves had been cleared away in hopes that snakes and other critters would keep their boundaries a little farther away. Abby shuddered as she looked at the area where Liz had once used her quick thinking by putting a bullet into a copperhead. Anyway, Samuel had reassured her that all slithering things would be looking for a winter home soon, and Abby was adamant that nothing would find a home at her school.

A newly dug cellar was also in the schoolyard. Mrs. Perkins, as a dutiful citizen of Fort Worth, was insistent that the school have one. "We must provide adequate shelter for the students," declared the civic-minded woman. Abby could still picture Mrs. Perkins as she stood there with her shoulders squared and chin held high.

Mrs. Perkins provided any funds needed to complete the project. Rumor had it that she had lost a child to a tornado that came through years ago and was most pleased once the shelter was complete. Days ago when Luke had driven some supplies out to her from his mother's mercantile, she chatted on and on about it. Mrs. Perkins really was a fine person, just a little lonely, but she involved herself with the folks of the town from birth to death and anything in between. She also said that she would donate a quilt to keep in the dirt shelter, just in case.

Samuel and Smithy had dug in the clay dirt for hours each day to get it completed. Abby heard the picks and shovels day after day. Finally, Pastor Parker and Jackson came to help. The men were covered with sweat and loose dirt caked on their bodies. On the last day, the men scooped the dirt into the back of a wagon and hauled it off. Samuel thought it was large enough for a dozen or so little ones to hide out for a short spell.

Smithy eventually brought a roof he had made to cover the hole. The shelter was easy to open for the schoolchildren, with a simple lock inside to keep the roof from blowing off. Abby thought the storm cellar looked like doors on a nondescript mound of dirt.

Abby looked back through the short path under the huge shady oak tree by the schoolyard. She saw a new outdoor privy with three doors. Jackson was proud of the three-hole outhouse he had built. "No excuse to be out here wasting time," he had told Abby as he swung the hammer. Each citizen of the new Fort Worth community was happy to help make the school ready.

A swing Abby had never noticed hung from the branch of Pastor Parker's ageless pecan tree. "I wonder who put that up," she murmured to herself when a lively red squirrel shook its tail and scampered up the back side of the old tree. Soon the rodent would be on the hunt for his winter supplies.

The last item on Abby's list was the water pump. The well had good fresh water in it. She worked the handle up and down, but it was difficult to get even a drop. She pumped and pumped, but the only moisture she could produce was the sweat on her brow. She made a mental note to have the older boys get it primed each day.

Satisfied with what she saw outside, Abby walked to the porch and lifted her skirt slightly to allow her feet easy access to go up the few steps. Abby saw Luke heading her way with a paintbrush and bucket of white paint.

Abby would have been proud of the young man even if he hadn't been her cousin's child. He was smart and responsible. He would do a fine job on the steps leading to greater knowledge.

"Hey, Miss Abby," Luke said, out of breath. "I finished my chores for Maw at the mercantile. I didn't forget about you. A promise is a promise!"

Abby saw Luke's precious smile. It was finally coming back after the death of his great-grandpa. Luke and his great-grandfather, Lucas, had always lived together at the family timber mill. They had been inseparable since Luke could toddle around. Building fence, sitting on the porch, and fishing were daily activities for the two Lukes. Losing his father and then his great-grandfather less than two years later had been rough. Welcoming a new man into the family, even one he was already fond of, couldn't have been a seamless adjustment for Luke.

"Luke," Abby said, "thank you for putting the final coat of paint on the steps. I know you've already had a busy day." It was important to praise her students and let them know she was aware of their participation and willingness to help out.

He dipped his brush in the bucket and got to work. Luke's dog, Bear, had already found some late morning shade under the stoop. "Miss Abby?" Luke called as she was about to enter the doorway.

"Yes, Luke."

"I hurried so I could go down to the river again with some of the other boys." He never looked away from his paintbrush as he spoke. "They were talkin' about the big fish in the river. Gonna get me one," Luke said with excitement and anticipation.

Abby stopped to hear Luke's story. "Exactly where is this, Luke?" she asked with concern.

"The bridge over Trinity River." Luke kept painting. He was careful to do a neat job, but in a hurry to get to the waterhole.

"Just be careful, Luke. We have heard dangerous stories about that river. And is that the bridge they call broken?"

"Maybe." He was vague. "It's just maybe a little rough in the spring when it floods." Luke had now covered one side of the porch rails with fresh white paint. He leaned over the rail to catch a drip. "Don't worry none about it. Ain't gonna letcha down. I will do yuh a nice job on this here porch."

He glanced up at Abby and went right back to the paint bucket. He grinned mischievously as he teased his teacher with poor grammar.

"I'm sure you will. Remember safety first and fun second. Luke, please be careful at the river." Luke nodded at Abby.

Abby knew Luke felt loved, but at times he must have wondered just how many mothers were watching over him.

※　※　※

Her classroom organization well in hand, Abby allowed herself a few days off to help Megan and Emma tend the abundant garden. She enjoyed the feel of working with her hands, and she likened the growth of the vegetables to the growth she envisioned with her students as she nurtured them to what she expected to be a bumper crop of learning.

Soon she was back in her classroom putting the finishing touches on an arithmetic lesson. She hung a quilt made from her favorite pattern on the wall. The plaid fabric featured a strip of small berries along the border, a remnant from a childhood dress. The quilt had been sewn when she was almost grown and it brought back sweet memories of her youth. In addition, the pattern was useful in reinforcing a lesson in arithmetic, especially for the girls.

Abby heard the door open. Thinking the wind had been the culprit, she started walking back to shut it and was startled when a young Indian girl with shining black hair stepped through the doorway. They stared at each other for a moment until Abby asked slowly, hoping the child understood English, "And just who are you, my dear?"

"I'm Little Dove." Her soft voice expressed some timidity as though unsure of her reception, yet her long, dark lashes covered self-assured, jet black eyes.

As she took a few steps into the room, her skirt jingled with colorful beads tied on a leather string around her waist. Abby saw that her skirt was made from soft animal skins and her shirt was a cotton print. She carried something bulky in her arms.

"Are you the new teacher?" Little Dove looked expectantly at Abby, who was still recovering from the surprise visit.

"Yes. Yes, I'm Miss Wilkes, the new teacher in Fort Worth." With another question of her own, she asked, "How did you know about the school?"

Little Dove answered by telling her story tonelessly. "My mother married a white man—so I know English as well as my mother's tongue—and we lived in the hills with her people until the soldiers came. Then my father was killed. Ma and I were sold as slaves, passed around by thieves and outlaws mostly."

The Indian girl dropped a bundle onto the teacher's desk and resumed her story. "Ma died awhile back and mostly the men left me alone if I kept food plentiful and hid out."

Abby stepped closer. She nodded her head for the girl to continue.

Little Dove licked her lips and lowered her dark lashes. "The men who kept me are the two who killed your grandfather. Ranger Tex told me."

Abby stared in disbelief as she relived the feelings of loss she had experienced at the hands of the despicable men. She immediately felt a sense of protection toward this young girl who had known ugliness firsthand. For someone who had lived a life of horrific loss and tragedy, she seemed sweet and trusting.

"Mr. Tex found me when the Rangers came to the camp. He told me the bad men were dead. He said I should come with him and go to school. He wanted to bring me here, but first I said I could come alone," the young girl said. "Then he said he was a good man and I could trust him. I believed him."

Little Dove opened her belongings and revealed a beautifully pieced quilt with a black check and pumpkin-colored border. She unfolded it to reveal her few possessions.

"The Rangers burned the camp where they found me. This is all I have left. The Ranger, Tex, said I should not waste any more time."

Little Dove sat at the desk as though ready for her first lesson.

Abby stood, taking it all in. Finally, she found some words.

"This is a lovely quilt. Did you make it?" Abby came close enough to touch the softness of the much loved fabric.

"My mother made it for me. She said it was not woven like an Indian blanket but that she could use the same design. I know how to sew," she declared.

Abby remembered the account of the fire that took the life of Liz and Megan's parents. The two girls were found huddled together with only an appliquéd quilt, a treasure that had survived a tragedy, the only memento from their early life. Abby smiled at Little Dove and placed her hand on her shoulder.

"I would love to have you in class when we start in a few days. I think you will make an excellent student. How did you get here? Did you walk?"

She nodded her head as she looked at her pretty, new teacher. "Three days. I slept three nights in the trees."

"Oh," Abby exclaimed. "Why . . . in trees?"

"So the night animals wouldn't find me. Now I will stay in the school and be comfortable with my quilt."

"Oh," Abby said again, blinking her eyes. She wondered if she herself would have had the fortitude and resourcefulness this child had.

"Let's see if we can find you a place to sleep that will be a little bit more comfortable than a tree or the classroom." Abby paused to think. "My house is already too crowded, but I want you to meet my friend Anna. Let's go find her."

Little Dove gathered her quilt of belongings and stood to follow Abby trustingly.

Anna welcomed the two and invited them in for tea. She listened intently to Little Dove's incredible story and asked a few questions to fill in the gaps. Little Dove seemed almost unfazed by the violence she had already experienced in her young life. She was pretty and well-mannered, and her spoken words were better than many of her soon-to-be classmates.

"My husband, Pastor Parker, and I have room for you and would enjoy your young company. We would be happy to offer you a place to live while you go to school this year. And as you can see, we live quite close to the school," Anna teased. They lived right next door.

Anna didn't need to wonder if her husband would be happy about the young girl staying with them. For a very long time, they had both wanted children. Maybe Little Dove was the answer to their prayers.

"Follow me and I'll show you your new room." Anna motioned to her spare bedroom.

Little Dove appeared to be amazed at all that had happened to her in a short time. Anna and Abby hoped she would be able to trust that she had come to good people who would look after her. They watched as she settled her quilt bundle on the bed and sat down looking it over.

Anna stood in the sitting room and asked Abby quietly, "Do you think those dirty men left her alone?"

"I pray to God they did. She said she cooked for them and tried to stay out of their way. She is so young. Maybe they saw her as a child, not worthy of their attention," Abby said.

Anna smiled and looked toward the room where the girl was settling in. She finally had a child in her home.

CHAPTER 5

The customers cleared out of the mercantile and Liz finally had a moment to rest. It had been a busy morning and she was tired. But she looked around with satisfaction. She liked the way she had moved things around in the store. The place was no longer a reminder of the past but a testament to going ahead. The merchandise had been rearranged, blood-stains from the shooting had been scrubbed clean, and new curtains hung.

The days after the robbery that resulted in her grandfather's death were a blur of grief and rage. But Grandpa Lucas's almost final words before he left this earth for heaven were, *Marry Thomas, child. You need each other.* And because it was Thomas she turned to in her desperation, she knew Grandpa was right. She told Thomas she was ready to celebrate the gift of life and move ahead with their wedding.

She sat for a moment, thinking of all that had happened since. Then her eyes glimpsed the clock. Two in the afternoon! No wonder she was tired. She was hungry, too, she realized.

She glanced out the window and her mouth curved up in a smile. Thomas. He was on the sidewalk out front. He looked through the window as he passed by with a basket carried low in one hand. The door jangled as he opened it and he smiled at his first and only love.

"Are you hungry?" he asked as he reached her and bent to kiss her cheek.

She wrapped her arms around his neck and said, "Yes, thank you! Did Megan or Emma send lunch?"

Thomas led Liz over to a small table and two chairs on a neatly woven dark rug. He moved a checkerboard to the side and set the basket down.

"Looks like I brought it," he joked. "Naw, I caught Emma with the basket. She was taking one over to the school for Abby, too. Take a break and eat with me."

Thomas stretched one long leg out to the side of the table and bent the other to go under the table. "Looks like you had a wagonload of customers again today."

He took a bite of a biscuit that melted in his mouth, silently grateful for the beautiful women in his new family and their cooking talents as well. He was so lost thinking about the wonderful flavors he was tasting, he forgot that he was having a meal with his wife.

"Yes." She smiled. "It has been busy with the last shipment of canning supplies and nails." Liz giggled as she watched him fade away with each new bite. "How long has it been since you had one of Emma's biscuits?"

"Just this morning. I don't know which I like more . . ." He paused and with a teasing look added, "waking up with you or having breakfast at the table of the Mailly women."

He thought back to those days when he and his best friend, Caleb, left their home after they finished school. They were young bucks ready to seek their fortune in the world. They accidentally found the Riverton Timber Mill and Lucas Mailly. Lucas hired them on immediately.

Caleb and Thomas both saw Lucas's granddaughter Elizabeth at the same time. She was standing on the porch, by the pillars with her cat. Thomas would never forget that picture as long as he lived. He was the quiet one of the two, so naturally Caleb claimed her first. They were married after a whirlwind courtship and Luke was born a year later.

Thomas had to be content as an extended part of the family and watch his best friend enjoy life. He was able to be good friends with little

Luke and better than a son-in-law to Lucas. He loved the older man with all his heart and continued to carry his dream out to Texas.

When Caleb died in a lumber accident, Thomas mourned for his friend, but the flame he'd held for Liz never extinguished. During the wagon train ride west, Thomas decided not to wait any longer to court Liz with the intention of asking her to marry him. Being wedded wasn't as easy as he thought it would be. Liz was headstrong and had her own opinions. But that was part of her, and Thomas could adjust. Though the quiet type, Thomas would always do what was best for the family.

Thomas easily fell into the shoes of Lucas and Caleb after their deaths. He was the sole rooster in the henhouse of the Mailly women, and they respected him.

✳ ✳ ✳

Liz smiled and stood to kiss his cheek. She then took a glass and as she started to pour some milk for the two of them she had to stop and place a hand on her husband's shoulder to steady herself. She closed her eyes for a moment as the room circled fast around her.

Several weeks had gone by since the wedding. The fall harvest of gardening was in full steam and Liz had lost track of time. Being a wife again, running the new mercantile, and pushing through her grief again had her emotions on overload. Now, she was feeling the brunt of it.

"Liz," Thomas kindly reminded her, "you work too hard and don't eat and drink enough during the day. Here, have a seat. Try a biscuit and drink this milk." He pushed it closer to his bride.

"I'm fine. I just got up too quickly. I didn't feel like eating this morning and now I'm famished."

Thomas saw her color coming back and dismissed any concerns he had.

"Well, Thomas," Liz began. She nibbled at her bread. "Since the crops and gardens are doing so well, we will continue to have delicious meals gracing our tables through the winter."

Liz swallowed and sipped some more milk. "Everyone in the area has ordered and picked up extra canning jars and supplies. They are putting up more jars than they ever have before!"

Thomas listened as he ate.

Liz picked up a pickle from last year's crop in Louisiana. "Katie Longmont said that she had already put up over one hundred jars."

"Put up?" Thomas asked.

"Yes, that's the way they say it here. They put the jars up on a shelf and count them. So they would say I have ten put-ups."

"Just a way to state the completed number of the canning jars," Thomas replied. He nodded and wiped his milk mustache from his real mustache. "Did any newspapers come in with the freight?"

Liz stood and picked up several. Her grandfather had always had numerous newspapers in his mail. Thomas had enjoyed them as well as Liz, and she had no intention to cancel any after his death.

Thomas pushed back and placed one leg on the now empty chair and snapped open the paper from Austin.

"Looks like the governor's mansion is almost finished. I saw it when I was down that way. It is really grand with tall white pillars in the front. Looks like a Southern plantation!"

Liz gathered up the remains of lunch and went back to the counter where her order ledgers and catalogs were. She left Thomas to enjoy his various papers in peace.

It seemed like only minutes had gone by when Thomas scooted both feet under the table. His brow was crossed as he read and his hand went back and forth over his chin.

"What is it?" Liz was concerned with what he might have read. "What does it say?" She stopped to listen.

"This isn't good. Lucas was right!" Thomas kept his eyes on the page and continued to read the article. "It's about the election for president." Liz went to read over his shoulder and her eyes scanned the news.

She thought about what she had read. Stephen A. Douglas coveted the Democratic nomination for 1856, but his reputation had been badly tarnished by the ongoing violence in Kansas. Douglas's proposal on the Kansas-Nebraska Act shattered both the letter and spirit of the 1820

Missouri Compromise. The debate over the future of slavery became more violent than ever. The most immediate and deadly reaction to Douglas's act was that it opened the floodgates for both sides to pour men, money, and guns into the territory to influence the vote on slavery. In his place, the party turned to James Buchanan, who could carry the Southern votes.

The Republicans were running their first presidential campaign and chose a Western explorer, John Frémont, nicknamed "The Pathfinder." They ran their campaign on the repeal of the hated Kansas-Nebraska Act. The Republicans took every opportunity to blame the Democrats for the horrors of "Bleeding Kansas."

The American party, dubbed the "Know Nothings," nominated Millard Fillmore.

The Democrats were strong in the South and the Republicans in the North. The election was mirroring the sectional feelings of the day. It seemed the election was sure to bring a weak president to leadership in a badly divided nation.

Thomas and Liz read on to another article. "Bleeding Kansas" was in bold print as the title. Another read, "Strife Continuous Following the Act of 1854."

Liz continued to read the article and sorted in her mind as she went. Things were working out as planned in Nebraska as a free state, but not in Kansas. It was to be a slave state but influential outsiders decided to make an example of Kansas. Abolitionists in the North organized and funded several thousand settlers to move to the Great Plains and vote to make it a free state. Topeka and Lawrence were settlements where antislavery prevailed while pro-slavery groups formed in the towns of Leavenworth and Atchison. With violence and intimidation, "Border Ruffians" pushed through pro-slavery legistlation in territorial elections. Most of these ruffians were poor Missourians, who were sympathetic to slaves who crossed over the border to Kansas.

Many tense situations erupted into violence that could easily be regarded as the opening shots of a nation divided. Violent clashes became commonplace as lynching, murder, and burning replaced popular sovereignty. Federal authorities, including resident Franklin Pierce, were helpless to stop the escalating bloodshed.

Governor John Geary was pleading with the Missourians to return home after a raid in Lawrence, Kansas. John Brown and four of his sons, along with an army of men, dragged five pro-slavery settlers who were completely innocent from their homes along Pottawatomie Creek and, in front of their families, shot and hacked them to death with scythes, weapons once favored by medieval knights. Brown and his sons evaded capture. More than two hundred people had died in the border wars in Kansas in the last two years.

Liz gasped as she read this story and Thomas stopped reading to look at her.

"This is horrible," she exclaimed. "This has to stop! We are a civilized nation." Now worried she asked, "Will any of this reach us?"

Thomas studied her for a moment. "I'm not sure. Our freight comes from Louisiana. But I'm sure that anything coming from Kansas City or maybe Saint Louis could be in jeopardy of attacks."

"By our own people?" Liz exclaimed. "This is crazy! I think everyone has lost their minds. I don't understand the violence that some people resort to."

"Only time will tell how this plays out. I do feel like it will get worse, a lot worse, before it gets better." Thomas was worried as to how it would affect them. Not only could their businesses be hurt but also the family they loved.

"I'm tired of this hurt and pain being dealt out by ruthless people. Didn't we go far enough to be excluded from the violence? Haven't we been through enough?" Her voice quavered. Thomas just gave her a hug and was silent. He wasn't sure that anyone was far enough away.

CHAPTER 6

Abby had one last home visit but wasn't quite sure how to go about it. She really shouldn't depend on Samuel to help out with every detail. She felt it was her responsibility, after all.

Maybe the Parkers could help with her dilemma. As the pastor, he was always making visits to his flock. Abby was pleased with this idea. She would make a stop at Anna Parker's on her walk home to inquire about Parker's church visits.

The grant money for her school was within her grasp if she could only get at least twelve students. She hoped to finalize the paperwork and send it with Tex. He would go south soon and could take it then. But first she would need to make that call on Peter Graham, her twelfth student.

Assured that all was in order, Abby closed the door to her classroom and proceeded on her errand. As she rounded the corner of the church, she saw the side door ajar and caught a glimpse of Pastor Parker and Jackson going inside. She wondered what they were up to and was curious, but she had her own schedule to attend to and this mystery would just have to wait.

Anna Parker was coming out of her home next to the church. Anna had always been thin and slightly taller than Abby, but today she seemed to have a fullness about her. She greeted Abby with her sweet voice.

"Abby, hello," she said with a wave. "Please wait so I can visit with you as we walk down to the mercantile. Aren't you going that way?"

Abby noted the dampness around Anna's temples. It was warm and Anna had worked up a sweat. Anna was drying her hands on an almost clean white apron when she suddenly said, "Oh, I forgot to take my apron off in my haste to get to the store." Anna chided herself and scratched at a dried tomato seed that had stuck on one pink stain. "That's all well, I guess," she continued. "Everyone is busy over a hot stove." Anna was referring to the canning that all of Tarrant County was involved with.

"How is Little Dove?" Abby asked.

"She is just wonderful," Anna replied joyfully. "I can't believe she has been here only a short time and has adjusted so beautifully. It really is a blessing to have her."

The women walked up the stairs to the wooden boarded sidewalk. They passed some empty buildings that the army had left behind.

Both women smiled and Abby placed her hand on Anna's arm. Anna was the sweetest, most considerate woman that she had ever met. She could learn a lot from her. They had formed an instant friendship.

"Oh, Anna, it is good to see you and hear how you and Little Dove are getting along. I so want her to be happy. Do you think Tex found her in time, before much damage was imposed on her? I just can't imagine the life she has had, being a slave to that horrific bunch of outlaws." Abby shook her head and searched the eyes of her friend, hoping to hear good words.

"God is good," Anna said as she placed her hand over Abby's. "He is truly good. I do believe she is untouched. Her spirit is kind and she is so accepting. She learned a lot with a parent from each world and I do believe her first several years were in a loving environment. I'm so thankful that Tex found her and sent her to us."

"Do you think she will stay indefinitely?" the teacher asked.

"I don't know where she would go or why she would leave. We have told her that we want her." Anna paused with a glisten in her eyes. "We want her to be ours." Anna had lost several babies over the years. Only her God knew why she couldn't carry them to term. She was a healthy woman and maybe someday she would be blessed.

"Good!" Abby stated with a confident firmness. "She will do well in my classroom."

With that settled, the women continued on to the general store discussing the matters of the day.

"Anna, I still have one family to visit. The Grahams? I heard there was a boy. Do you know his whereabouts, how old he is, or anything about his family?"

Anna stopped again to think. "Yes, yes I do. The son is Peter. His father is, forgive me, a crazy old kook. They live close to the river in a bend of trees. The cabin is unkempt and he is strict with Peter. We had barely arrived at the settlement when Heath went out to see about them and he scarcely escaped with his life. The wife had died and the disturbed man had laid out her body on the table in the house. Heath wasn't sure how many days she had been there before he arrived, but the smell was already horrible."

"Oh," Abby gasped, as her hand went to her throat. "Where was the child, Peter?"

"He was there, huddled in the corner. Finally, Heath got the man convinced to bury his wife. Heath dug the hole, read Scripture, and said a prayer. Suddenly the man went crazy and started to claw at the grave with his bare hands, crying and screaming. Then he started to attack Heath. Almost knocked him in the grave and tried to choke him!"

Abby's eyes were wide as she listened to Anna's story. "How old would you expect Peter to be now?"

"Maybe twelve or thirteen. We don't see them often. He did come to town with Peter right after Liz opened the mercantile. Peter just quietly sat in the wagon while his pa went inside for supplies."

Abby was thoughtful as she asked, "Do you think we can get him to school? He would be my twelfth student."

"The house is within walking distance, even if it is a good piece down the road. I can walk out with you if you like."

Abby detected hope in Anna's voice. It sounded like the two of them could possibly go without bothering the men about it. She would have to think this through.

"Thank you, Anna; I will let you know what I decide."

The two ladies reached the door of the mercantile and pushed inside to the normally friendly environment. Liz looked tired and upset as she straightened things for closing.

"Looks like you were busy today," Abby said to her cousin.

"Shoppers can be messy at times, I guess," Anna said cheerfully.

They both looked at Liz and then at each other. They were both getting the same idea about Liz not being herself. She looked pale and just plain tuckered out. At the same time, they both asked, "Liz, are you all right?"

Liz looked to both women and wasn't able to hold back any longer.

"Yes and no." She sighed. "I don't know what is wrong with me today. I woke up nauseated, then starved and hurried to work without a thing to eat. I was so busy today with the freight arriving and the orders being picked up or readied for Luke to deliver. Then Thomas came by late with my lunch basket. I was famished and had a slight dizzy spell."

Liz stopped to think for a moment as both women were staring at her. She continued on, noticing their intent looks toward her.

"Thomas had several newspapers that came and they were full of death and all types of unrest between the North and the South with words of war. Kansas is all in an upheaval and people have been killed. Our president seems helpless in the matter and the governor has sent out a plea for it to stop. It's just like Grandpa predicted." Liz swiped at the tears on her cheeks defiantly. She hated any sign of weakness in herself. "It has just overwhelmed me. I've allowed it to get the best of me."

"Have you had a fever at all?" Anna asked.

"You are a little pale," Abby chimed in.

"I'm not sure. It did warm up some today. I was too busy to tell."

"Liz, I'm not sure I would know if it was me, but . . . but, do you think you could be expecting?" Abby slowly got the question out that she and Anna both wanted to ask.

Liz was stunned. "It never crossed my mind that I would have a child in this marriage after all those barren years with Caleb. Thomas and I never discussed it. I don't even know if he wants any children. We both just assumed Luke was all."

Abby brought Liz a stool and urged her to sit down.

"Do you think—" Liz paused. "And so soon?"

Abby and Anna watched Liz cautiously. She seemed disbelieving at the possibility.

"We won't tell a soul." Anna patted the shaken Liz. "Maybe it's just a bug or your body reacting to the things . . . in our life." Anna fumbled with the excuse.

"Yes, we will give it some time," Abby added, "some much needed time."

✳   ✳   ✳

Emma watched as the cowboys approached the back of town close to her house. They were a rough looking bunch. The dirt they stirred up seemed to follow them like a shadow. She had just stepped away from the house for a moment and now she couldn't even tell which direction was home. She pulled her apron over her mouth so she could breathe more easily. Even the sun was having a hard time gathering the strength to shine through the dust storm that had arrived with the riders.

Emma could hear the horses as they snorted the dust from their own nostrils and panted. They were close, hooves were clomping. She wasn't sure if she was in danger or not and covered her face from the impending dirt.

"Ma'am." Emma heard a husky voice and slightly lowered her apron so she could see and still keep the dirt from her eyes. Visibility was a little better now, though dirt was starting to settle in her hair and everywhere else.

"Oh, wonderful, just wonderful," the young cantankerous woman murmured.

"Ma'am?" the dusty cowboy repeated.

The horse he was on was skittish and wanted to rear up. The wrangler held the reins tightly for control. Emma cooed soft words and reached up to stroke the animal's neck. She looked into her eyes and ignored the rider. The horse calmed immediately; her breathing was less labored and her hooves quit prancing.

"Ma'am, that was dangerous." The same cowboy spoke.

Emma ran her hand down the front leg of the horse. It quivered a little from her touch as the muscles cooled down. Emma's green eyes blinked a few times as the dirt settled in the corners of the shining emeralds. She raised her head and finally spoke.

"Not as foolish as it is to mistreat the animals you depend on." Sparks flew from her as she chastised the man. "You keep working her like this and you won't have a horse to ride. Can't you tell her leg is hurt?"

The man dismounted and stood next to Emma. The other eight or so cowboys watched intently. Emma didn't appear to mind being outnumbered by rough looking cowboys, who watched with interest to see the outcome of this match. She checked the mouth of the horse where the bit was. The corners of the horse's mouth were raw and bruised. "You've been jerking her bit, too."

"Lady," he demanded, "what gives you the right to tell me how to treat my pony? She's a might frisky—like you, no disrespect intended—and needs a little jerk on her reins now and then!"

"If I had reins in my hands, I'd show *you* what it was like." Emma lashed out at the cowboy without fear or intimidation. "What gives you the right to come riding in here full speed ahead like a gang of outlaws? Thundering through, kicking up dust as though you were out on the open prairie."

Emma was on the toes of her boots with hands on her hips. She was trying to be at eye level with him but couldn't.

He shook his head and relaxed a little, realizing that this young lady couldn't really be a threat. She just took him off guard. He didn't have a clue that anyone was about until the dust settled and there she was using her apron to cover her face.

"Ma'am, let's start over." He licked his lips and took his cowboy hat off and held it with both hands. "We apologize for almost running you over. We just needed to get to town before dark set in. My men and I need a bath and some food. We've been herding two hundred head of ornery longhorns for weeks and we all," he paused, "horses included, need a little attention."

Emma placed her heels flat on the ground and looked the cowboys over one by one. She walked to each horse and whispered to it as she rubbed its velvety nose and neck. She loved horses. In some ways, they were preferable to people. She glanced at the cowboys and an idea began forming in her mind. She thought quickly. Was life about to get just a little exciting?

Emma was small in size and had brown hair that shone like spun gold in the sun. At least, when it wasn't full of dust. It had a lot of curl like her sister Abby's, but that was the only thing they shared.

Abby's prudence and relentless pursuit of perfection drove Emma crazy. She longed for some variety in her dull life. Lately she felt like she was on a road to nowhere. Her cousins Liz and Megan as well as her sister Abby all had plans for their life in their new Fort Worth home. Emma was tired of following someone else's dreams and, frankly, being bossed around by the well-meaning bunch.

Emma was bored from the gardening and canning that had gone on for so many days that she had lost count. Pick, wash, slice, cook. Boil the canning jars and lids. Fill them with the seasoned or sugary mixtures. Carefully apply lids. Boil again.

Each morning Liz and Thomas appeared from their room for breakfast, then they went on their way, Liz to the mercantile and Thomas to his duties. Emma wasn't exactly sure what he did all day. Yes, he did have the freight business and helped Liz at the mercantile occasionally. Thomas made sure that Luke did the deliveries and that they were all toeing the line. But they had it all worked out just as well before he became king of their domain.

Abby was busy with her employment at the school, which left her and Megan to run the house.

Cleaning, cooking, and taking lunch each day to Abby and Liz was her excitement for the day. Her parents had slaves who had more of a future than she did. In fact, this was exactly what they were doing back home in Mississippi. Nellie had brought her lunch each day in a basket!

Emma did love to cook and was quite good at it. She never lacked for any compliments when she did take the notion to cook. Back home in Mississippi she cooked when she wanted to, when books and sewing got boring. She had tried to get involved with her father's horse business. Emma loved to ride and the animals responded well to her. She had a knack with the large creatures. But, since she was a female, her father never took her seriously and continually sent her back to the house. Many times, she snuck out to the stables, where she learned a lot from Isaac, their slave who tended the horses.

She knew that she should be grateful for a family who loved her and had food on the table, and she was, but what was there to look forward to? Would her life on the frontier ever have more to it than the everyday routine?

It just wouldn't do to be stuck inside all day. Emma longed for the outdoors, fresh air, and a little excitement. Another thing she needed was money of her own. Everything she needed or asked for was supplied. She had to find a way to earn her own way. She hadn't known what she was looking for until she lowered her apron from her face. Part of what she wanted was looking down at her. So she said,

"I can provide a good meal and a bath for each of you . . . one dollar and you each get clean, hot water. Your horses can get their wounds cleaned and cared for, as well as hay and oats for the night. If you need a place to sleep, that's extra. The horses are worth more than you and your men. They will cost two-fifty each."

Emma didn't expect the men to take her offer. It was highway robbery. The price she quoted was more than double the usual charge for these services. The slim cowboy that she had gone nose to nose with was silent. He looked to his men. They hadn't moved a muscle during the whole exchange. Not a one of them even had a finger on his gun. They just watched in amazement as the two went at it.

"Well, that's the first time I've been robbed without a gun in my ribs." He chuckled. "How good is the cooking?" He pretended to gain some bartering power with Emma.

"The best you've ever had," Emma told him confidently. "Be back here in one hour," she snapped and whirled to leave.

Emma couldn't believe what she had just done. Luck had turned her way. She spoke with confidence that she had never displayed before and she was going to make some money on her slave labor. She just needed a little help and hoped Megan and Luke would be willing.

And they were.

For the next three hours Emma and Megan prepared roasted chicken with all the trimmings, in between heating water on the stove and in their fancy bathhouse.

When the women had moved into the captain's home, they had discovered lavish bathing facilities in a small shed behind the main house. So far, only the family had used it. Some of the Rangers had joked about it being a moneymaker, but no one had ever taken it seriously until now. Megan couldn't believe what Emma had done but was willing to help. Luke even agreed when he heard that he could rake in ten cents a head. He even chased down a chicken or two and took care of the towels at the bathhouse.

After the men were fed and bathed, they sat out on the porch with coffee and dessert. They discovered that their money was well spent. Emma's peach cobbler alone was worth the price of admission.

Emma was standing on the porch with the coffeepot in her hand and almost thirty dollars in her apron pocket when the rest of her family arrived home for the evening.

※　※　※

Megan looked at her family and realized it was time for round two of the evening meal.

"Emma." Megan's fatigue was evident in her tone.

"Yes?" Emma answered. She had stopped long enough to realize she was worn to the bone.

"What do we have left to feed our own family?"

"I've got some soup on the back burner. I kept putting potatoes and chicken in as we went. It should be enough with the bread and peach cobbler. I kept one pan back." Emma chuckled. "The big cowboy said he would give me five dollars for it."

Megan wiped her face with the apron that was completely saturated and plopped into a chair. "Good, because I couldn't cook one more pan or pot of anything!" She let out a breath and rested her head on the back of the chair. "I've boiled enough water to last me a good while."

Liz and Abby came through the back door. They had seen all the cowboys earlier and Luke had told them that the men were paying for their dinner and using the bathhouse to clean up. Luke flashed the money he had earned and headed back to the barn.

"I need to help Luke and put a tincture on one of the horses," Emma said to Megan. "If you don't mind, I will go out now."

Abby saw what needed to be done and went straight to work.

"Megan, Liz, you two have a seat," Abby interrupted. "I will get food on the table. Emma, when you see about the horse, tell Thomas his supper is ready, please. He is on the porch with the cowboys."

Emma went to the cabinet where she had a mixture of lavender and moonshine. It would have been better if she could have let it sit in the sun for three days. She didn't have that much time, so she had been letting it simmer on the stove. She pulled the petals, leaves, and twigs from the liquid where it was cooling and put it in a cloth.

"This should work," she decided and went out the door to the barn. The horse shook her head and nickered at Emma. She wanted to see the young lady who spoke her language and had her head turned as far as it would go. Emma spoke a soft greeting and the horse nuzzled her. She ran her hand down the shoulder of the front leg. When the horse flinched, she knew where to apply the tincture. She held it firmly to the spot with one hand and used the other to rub under the horse's jaw. She could feel the horse relax.

"Good girl," she whispered. "If you don't resist the medicine, you will heal quicker." Emma secured the mixture and used her hands to check the horse for other injuries. She discovered that this was one fine animal, worthy of so much more than just herding cattle. Emma wanted this horse. She had a strange feeling that this horse was meant to be hers. She heard footsteps behind her and knew the tall cowboy had walked into the stalls even before he asked, "How is she?"

Emma looked his way and now saw a cowboy who looked much younger than he had awhile ago. With the dirt washed away he was more pleasant in looks and demeanor. "Your master seems to be human after all," she whispered to the horse. "She will be fine but I would recommend that she not be ridden for a few days." Emma barely looked at the cowboy when she spoke. "Maybe you should leave her, let her get stronger. Thomas could help you with another horse."

"Hmmm. I do need a smart horse suitable for cattle driving; not just any would do. Not sure I would have any money for one after what we spent tonight." His snicker sounded like he'd been around horses a lot. The animal turned to look at her master.

"Maybe you should just sell her. I don't think she will be much good at working cattle, even in a few days." Emma hesitated and then said, "I could take her off your hands. I don't mind doctoring her." She held her breath and was hopeful, though she sensed the familiar lack of self-confidence return.

The cowboy poked his hands in his pockets. "I could consider that." He waited a moment, then turned to leave the barn.

Luke was finished with the hay and water and climbed down from the loft. "Miss Emma, I heard what you said. Would you really buy the horse?"

"Yes, Luke, I sure would." The horse nuzzled her again.

Thomas had taken his food out to the porch and was talking with the group of men who had become their paying guests. He learned that they had rounded up the longhorns from the hill country and driven them this far, hoping to herd them north to sell. The men reported that herding cattle was much harder than they expected and weren't looking forward to the rest of the trip. Part of the problem was they had no chuck wagon or cook. They were young men on a whim, looking for easy money.

Thomas sat rocking, listening to them. They seemed like a good bunch of cowboys; they had just taken on more than they could handle.

The cowboys took turns eating, cleaning up, and watching the herd. Thomas and a handful of punchers watched as the last round of hands rode out to where the herd was grazing at a grassy spot about a mile out. The murmur of the animals settling down for the night could be heard in the not too far distance. Only a small cloud of dust could be seen against the setting sun.

"I have an idea," Thomas said as he swayed back and hooked a heel of his boot so that the chair stayed cocked back. "Would any of you like to stay on as cowpunchers for me? I've been looking to buy a herd. Thought I would have to round them up myself. I have some land up north and I'm itching to get it ranching."

He let the chair slow down. "I'll sure need help building corrals, barns, and a bunkhouse, and with branding and general cowboy work. Think on it tonight and let me know. We can talk out the details in the morning over breakfast."

"What will that cost us?" the big one asked.

They all laughed heartily and Thomas joined in. He had heard what Emma had charged for the work.

"Well, it's on me." Thomas grinned.

The cowboys walked out a ways and built a fire not far from the herd. They rolled out their blankets and went to sleep under an illuminated Texas sky.

Only Thomas and Luke now remained on the porch. Liz, Megan, and Emma had all turned in, exhausted. Abby had finished up in the kitchen and had even mixed up the dough to rise for the morning's cinnamon rolls.

Luke sat in one rocker while Thomas had moved to a straight-backed chair. Silence wasn't uncomfortable for either one. Luke had spent many evenings with Thomas, his grandfather, and his pa, Caleb, since he could remember. Now it was just the two of them left. At these times they especially missed the comforting smell of Lucas's corncob pipe. All the years of growing up as part of the fabric of the family's daily life helped Thomas naturally step into his role as Luke's new pa.

Luke started the slow conversation as his chair rocked back and forth.

"You gonna buy that herd?"

"I think it makes good sense. They're already here. I'm hoping at least half of the cowboys will hire on and we can get the ranch going."

The conversation stayed steady with the motion of his rocking chair.

"Will I stay here or go to the ranch?"

Thomas rocked and thought. "I would think that you should stay in town and start school. We would have to buck against your mom and Miss Abby. I would really like for you to be at the ranch but for now, I think school is the best place for you. Your mom and Abby would be upset if you came with me just now. Let's just give it some time. Stay up with your studies and I will get you to the ranch as soon as I can. Okay, buddy?"

"But I'm almost a man. I shouldn't be in school with the little kids."

Thomas hid a smile and considered his answer seriously. "Well, a rancher needs all the learning he can get, Luke. You need to read and write and cipher to be a good businessman."

Luke rocked. "I guess so."

"Did you fish today?"

Luke stopped and looked at his new father as excitement rolled out of him. He had had a full day of adventures and spoke eagerly about them. Thomas would be more interested than his ma, he figured.

"You wouldn't believe it. The catfish are as big as dogs. They lie around on the bottom just gettin' big. Of a mornin' we fish with our poles, but come afternoon we dive in from the bridge. We go down deep and grab 'em with our bare hands!"

"You what?" Thomas stopped and looked at Luke to see if he was serious.

"Yup, I didn't believe it either until today. I saw it!"

"Who was there?" Thomas asked.

"The boys come after their morning chores. Mr. DeJarnette was there today. He's been doing it since he was a kid. He was the only one that caught any this afternoon. You should have seen the size of that fish he pulled from the bottom with his bare hands!"

"You dive from the bridge?" Thomas repeated. "Headfirst?"

"Sure."

"How deep is that water?"

"Deep enough," Luke assured him.

"Son, never dive where it's shallow, you hear? Who knows about this?"

"All the guys learned from their pas, they said. They've been doing it for years."

"Do any of the women know that you did this today?"

"Yes sir, I talked with Miss Abby."

"Did she think you were fishing or diving?"

"I suppose fishing and swimming. I didn't know about the diving till I got there."

"Well, let's keep it that way. Your mother hasn't been herself." Though Thomas had been a fixture in the family since before Luke was born, he was still learning what it meant to be a husband . . . and pa. Should he tell Liz about Luke's adventures? Keep it with the "men"? He decided. "She doesn't need to worry over it. I will talk to Samuel and Jackson about it and see what they know."

"Oh, they know. They've done it too."

"You don't say." Thomas was really curious about this now. Thomas sat on the porch a good hour after Luke went to bed thinking about his day and the turn of events with the ranch.

"Lucas, ole buddy, we got our herd," he whispered.

CHAPTER 7

Liz was an accomplished seamstress. She wasn't quite up to Megan's caliber, but few were. But she was accomplished in her own right nevertheless.

She counted every stitch that went into a garment or a patchwork quilt top. One hundred and three stitches for a man's collar and twelve stitches per inch for a quilt. The stitches had to be even and straight or the fabric wouldn't lie smoothly; a man wouldn't feel comfortable when he worked.

Late afternoon and early evening was the ideal time to sew on the porch. The light streamed by at a perfect angle. The day had grown mostly silent, with just an occasional voice drifting by or a horse neighing for its evening oats. If the wind blew just right, she could hear Thomas's herd of cattle over the ridge. Liz felt herself go deep into her thoughts where she could sort things out. She thought about each family member and the direction she saw their paths taking them. It was at this time she decided which stitches needed to be plucked from the patchwork of life and which ones strengthened the family unit.

Some decisions could never be changed or turned around and she knew it was best to rebuke the tendency to second guess as quickly as possible. Some mistakes could never be fixed in sewing if not caught immediately and removed. Like stitches, decisions were made one at a time. And when that thread was pulled, it had to be done carefully and thoughtfully so that the integrity of the fabric wasn't harmed. For one thread leads to another, and picking out one could easily unravel another.

Thomas had bought the herd. It was a done deal. They would be heading out anytime. Throughout the day he had marched into the mercantile with his big smile requesting something else for the support wagon or chuck wagon. Food, blankets, matches, nails, pots, pans. Soon his wagon would resemble Skelly's and most likely, the peddler would envy its contents.

Liz knew without a doubt that Thomas held this ranch in his heart. Her grandfather and Thomas had it all planned before they left Louisiana. This wasn't a surprise to her. But she had the mercantile to operate and Thomas's ranch was a good day's drive away.

When they left Louisiana she knew she would run the mercantile and the family would ranch, but she didn't know she would marry the rancher! How could she keep the store and be a rancher's wife when it was so far away? As things were now, she could just run across the yard from the Mailly home and be at work each morning. That would be impossible if she lived outside of town on the ranch.

Yes, it would be a good while before she would be expected to live there. But the day would come and it was too late to pluck out either the stitch of marriage or the stitch of owning a ranch. She had said yes with a smile and a promise. She couldn't take that light in Thomas's eyes away when he talked about his dream unfolding as planned. Just that morning as they were waking up to a new day, he held her in his arms and said, "This is more than I have ever dreamed of." She could feel his flutter of excitement with each heartbeat as she leaned close to him.

"Liz," he said as he shifted to look at her, "I never knew what it was like to share a bed with a woman." He paused and smiled at her blushing. "You are a good sleeping partner. You don't take up much space, you sleep silent, and you don't pull the covers. And your kisses taste like sweet red grapes." He traced the curve of her lips with his finger.

Caleb had never said she was a good wife or a good sleeping companion. But Thomas was more expressive with his emotions. With each kind word, she fell more deeply in love with him.

She pushed the needle into a connecting seam and let her hands lie idle in her lap just as the beams of sunlight started shifting away into the evening.

She would just have to find a way to put her expert skills as a seamstress together to get this piece of patchwork to lie square. She leaned her head against the rocking chair and prayed for the knowledge to do so.

※　※　※

Thomas pulled on his leather chaps and buckled them into place, just as he had been doing every morning of his life, not just the last three days. He picked up his gun belt and pushed a handful of bullets into the empty loops. Thomas and Buck had practiced shooting a few rounds the evening before behind Emma's henhouse, sending her and her chickens into a flurry. Cinching the gun belt loosely over his hips and tying the leather straps around the thigh of each leg, he chuckled at the memory.

He felt good about each of the women settling into their roles in their new home. Now was as good a time as any to leave them and start building the ranch. Tex and Jackson as well as Samuel, Smithy, and Parker were in town, and the women could call on them when they needed to, although these women were quite capable of handling most anything that came up. The old, weathered Tex was always on hand. Jackson showed up often just to see what was going on or to eat a meal. Thomas was beginning to think Jackson was sweet on Megan. He respected the man and had no reason for concern if it were true, though he might ask Liz what she thought about it. She was always a step ahead of him in what was happening in the family, and had a way of softly herding them in the way they should go. Now he needed to learn this talent with his cattle.

Thomas had expected to build a house, barn, and corrals first. Then he would get his herd together. Taking care of the cattle was a full-time job of its own, let alone all of the building of the structures. But that's the way life is, he figured—grab it by the horns and go with it as it comes.

Buck and Clyde counseled with him and the three made a knowledgeable group. They were good at setting a plan into action. First they needed a chuck wagon and a man who could cook. That was the biggest mistake the boys had made previously: can't work like a cowboy without good grub.

They also needed fresh horses. They had almost run the ones they had into the ground. Each cowpuncher needed at least two horses standing by to switch off with every few hours—horses that weren't too big, that were quick on their feet and not afraid of a longhorn when it got ornery.

Thomas had bought some good horses from the DeJarnette ranch and a half-grown cow dog from the latest litter. Mr. DeJarnette trained the pups and sold them for cow herding dogs. Thomas picked a sweet little female with the best skills and named her Maisy. She would be the first cowhand for the new Rolling M Ranch, named after Lucas Mailly.

Like all ranches in Texas, Thomas had registered his unique, new brand with the county. Smithy was working on making some branding irons for Thomas to pick up later that morning. The brand was a 90° angle with two letters intertwined: an "M" for Mailly was set inside the "L" for Lucas.

He had gotten one of those unexpected, sweet kisses from Liz when he showed her the brand. Just when he had grown used to being with her, he had to leave the house for the ranch. He didn't like that part of the plan. But then he couldn't expect her to abandon the mercantile to camp out with a bunch of cowboys.

With the cowboys who rode with Buck and Clyde and a wrangler from the Longmont's ranch he had enough hands. But he still needed a cook. As it was now, the hands would just take turns. No one looked forward to that! Thomas planned to ride out with the last supplies in the wagon and easily catch the herd as they were moving on to the ranch land at sunrise.

Liz heard the jingle of Thomas's spurs as he took the back stairs of the mercantile two at a time. She held the red bandana in her hand and tied the knot in the thread where she had just finished embroidering on the inside edge.

"I guess it's time," Thomas said as he lifted her to the bottom step where she was level to his face and kissed her. "I'll miss you."

She blinked and nodded to him. "I have a gift for you," she said as she showed him the bandana. "Here, on the edge, so you won't forget."

Thomas read the embroidered note. *I love you. Liz.* A tiny Texas bluebonnet embellished the words.

Thomas smiled. "I won't forget. But thank you. This certainly will help me breathe and keep the dust out."

She folded it into a triangle and double knotted it behind his neck. He swung her down with a smile and pushed his cowboy hat on his head. Liz grabbed a cotton bag and walked out the door with him to the wagon. Thomas leaped into the wagon. Maisy jumped in after him and he set her on the buckboard next to him.

"Be careful, Thomas. And have the time of your life!" She passed the bag to him and with a smile told him, "Some of Megan and Emma's home cooking."

Thomas slapped the reins on the rumps of the horses.

"Not sure I'll share this," he joked as the wagon rolled away.

Liz took a few steps to follow the wagon and saw a cloud of dust in the sky where the herd had been the days before. She watched until it was just a vast emptiness of dirt and wind.

※ ※ ※

As Thomas came over the ridge he saw the slow-moving herd encircled in a cloud of dust. He heard the crack of bullwhips as they snapped and sliced through the air. "Hey ya, yaa, yaa," the cowboys sang out as they circled their lariats and pushed the herd in the direction of the Rolling M Ranch.

Buck rode point, the coveted place while herding cattle. It was the only place where a cowboy didn't eat his share of dirt and dust. Next was the swing position, where the herd was the widest. After that the flank, three quarters to the back. And finally, the least desirable position to ride was the drag. Drag riders would become unrecognizable with inches of cattle dust caked on every part of their beings. Without a bandana to cover their nose and mouth they wouldn't be able to breathe. Their horses would snort dirt from their noses and blink cakes of dust to the corners of their eyes, almost blinding them at times. Low man rode drag; either he or the one who couldn't get along with the others.

The sounds coming from the traveling herd were a chorus of musical notes. Cowboys whistled, whips cracked, lariats whooshed, horses whinnied, cows brayed, Maisy yipped and barked in the back of the wagon, while riders sang out "move 'em out, head 'em up, hey yaw, hey yaws." It was music to Thomas's ears.

The cattle had been resting outside of town with the cowboys barely moving them while supplies were gathered for their journey. They were plenty ready to move out today in search of fresh grass and water. A fresh water creek, plenty wide, was only eight or nine miles away on the Longmont land. Thomas had paid for the rights to camp there the first night. They would cross over onto his land the next day where they would set up their permanent homestead.

The cowboying and ranching was becoming a natural part of him, and he relished the satisfaction it brought. The creak of his leather saddle as he shifted and gazed out on the land rolling on forever was what he loved and who he had become today. Out here on the range he felt closer to God and the earth than he had ever felt before. He started to whistle a hymn and praised God for His blessings.

The timber mill and logging business seemed a lifetime ago, although he knew he would use those skills to make bunkhouses for the ranch hands and a cabin for his family. He wanted to build Liz a big ranch house, but for now a cabin would have to do. Corrals and barns for his horses, with branding pens and gates for the cattle, needed to be built. He had asked around to the other ranches about the going rate of workers. Pay needed to be consistent among the ranches lest hands started hopping from one to another, hoping to make a little more dough, so he offered thirty dollars a month pay to his hands and one beef as a bonus at sale time. If workers did scout around for a different position it wouldn't be because of the pay.

Thomas had his saddle horse tied to the wagon and moved ahead of the herd, looking for that night's camp location. The chuck wagon had left tracks for Thomas to follow. As Thomas pulled his wagon into the camp a man, smaller in stature than his cowboys, came around the corner of the chuck wagon. Dark, curly, shaggy hair fell around his ears beneath a floppy hat. Thomas could see a fire burning, and sniffed delightful aromas drifting through the air to him.

The man turned to see who was coming into camp. He placed his gloved hand close to what Thomas guessed to be his gun belt. He climbed from the wagon and gave Maisy the command to jump down too.

"You must be Thomas Bratcher, head of this outfit. I met Clyde yesterday. He said I could stay and stir up some grub. If'n it suits you, maybe you'll take me on as your cook, sir."

Thomas put his hand out to greet the stranger with the raspy voice. Adenoids, maybe. His hand was on the small side but firm. "Yes, nice to meet you—" He waited for the man to give his name.

"Oh, Bet, call me Bet."

"Can you cook, Bet? Keep those cowhands fed and happy?"

"Yessir, I can."

"Well then, welcome to the Rolling M Ranch."

Bet nodded his head. "Mmmm. I wondered what brand I was riding with."

"Sure smells good. Guess you were quite a ways ahead of us."

"Yup, got started when it was still dark. No need waiting on them and getting in the way."

Good initiative, this Bet had. Thomas was approving.

Bet seemed to know what he was doing, so Thomas started to make camp. He strung up a line for the extra horses for when the wranglers showed up. He made the gear and other extra supplies accessible from the wagon.

Thomas turned when he heard a pig squeal. Looking around he saw it was tied to the cook's chuck wagon. "Is he our supper?" Thomas teased Bet.

"Nope, not tonight. I shot some prairie chickens, rolled out some dumplings, and Miss Emma in town sent along some of her peach cobbler for tonight."

Hmmm, Thomas thought, this isn't so bad.

Later in the day, the wrangler came in with the mustangs, and the sound of the herd could be heard at the creek. The cowboys drew straws to see who would take which shift for the night watch.

"Hey," one big cowboy said after supper. "Leave some of that cobbler for me. Emma said she sent it and I've tasted it all day as I ate that dust." He spoke as though he meant what he said.

"Hit the sack, boys. It won't be long before Buck yells to move 'em out."

※　※　※

At the end of the next day, the cowboys and the herd arrived at the property's grasslands. Thomas and Buck gave orders as to who would stay with the grazing herd and who would help start the building. Life fell into a rhythm at the Rolling M.

After several days, Bet was cleaning up the supper remains and brought a coffeepot to the campfire where the hands rested for the evening. He turned and went back to the chuck wagon.

"He ain't much on talk, is he?" one cowboy commented to another.

"Watch him walk," the other said.

"Leave him alone. As long as we have grub, what difference does it make?"

"Do you ever see him with his gloves off? That would tell us."

"Not that I recall."

"How can you tell in those baggy clothes?" another said as each hired hand put in his two cents' worth.

"I can," another said. "I can tell a woman when I see one and Bet is a woman."

"With that hair always in his face and the brim of that hat pulled down how can you tell?"

"Have you seen the eyes?" someone asked. "I have and them is surely female."

Thomas walked into the group to refill his tin cup. He stood and listened for a moment to find out what the conversation was about.

"Bet is a girl, Thomas. You hired us a lady chuck wagon cook." All the men looked at Thomas.

Thomas stood with one hand in his gun belt and the other with the coffee cup at his mouth. His eyes darted from around the crowd and landed on Bet.

That's it, Thomas thought. He knew something was off when he hired him . . . her. Well, this could certainly be interesting.

"Well, I'll be," Thomas slowly said as he watched the cook. "Fellas, I think you might be right."

"You gonna keep her?" the big cowboy asked, with a dessert bowl in front of him.

"Why not? *You* want Bet's job?" Thomas added.

"Nope, just wondered. Her secret is safe with me."

"Leave her alone, boys. Whatever her reason is, let her be. As much as she shoots for us to eat, you better think twice before upsetting our cook."

⁂ ⁂ ⁂

Thomas had turned the cattle out on the open range where they spread out, spending their days grazing freely. Once the corrals had been built and construction on the barns had begun, Buck announced it was time to bring in the herd, brand all the calves, and castrate the young bulls. Then they would turn them back out until the spring roundup.

Two ranch hands, Flip and Easy, had herded the strays together and were bringing them in for branding. The little heifers would be quickly branded then released to find their mommas and graze freely again. If these hands did a good job and the work continued to increase, they knew they would always have a job. Their boss seemed pretty good to work for and they liked Buck, the foreman. They still didn't have Bet figured out, but the food was good and plentiful. No whiskey in camp, Buck had told them when they hired on. He said to save it for the weekend.

The two hands saw a riderless palomino bolting across the open prairie land, a blur of black mane and tail streaming in the wind.

"Isn't that Thomas's horse?"

"Ya, boss man rode out on him today."

"I think we should leave these little doggies and go look for him."

As Buck rode over the ridge, he saw the unchecked palomino galloping like a bat out of hades, and without Thomas. He knew some of these horses were green, but to completely lose its rider and be hightailing frantically was something else. Buck pushed his pony into a gallop and let out a high-pitched whistle to the attention of Flip and Easy.

"Where's Thomas? Didn't he ride out on that runaway horse?" he hollered.

"Yup, we think so. Just saw the horse, but no boss man," Flip answered.

"Where was Thomas going and where did the horse come from?" Buck asked, searching the horizon.

Easy pointed to the area with the short trees. "Over that hill."

Buck reined his mount, which kicked up the dust as he rode away. Moving through the trees he heard a calf bawling and saw several scattered in the shade of the mesquite trees. Looking and listening, he heard nothing. He searched the ground for tracks and after a few minutes finally saw some. He got off his horse and pulled his pistol from the holster on the side of his leg.

Walking cautiously, he followed the tracks to the dirt ravine. Coming around the bend of trees he saw the slope leading to the ravine and there saw his friend lying motionless on the ground, blood running down his forehead and onto his cheek.

"Thomas," he called, looking around at the ravine one more time before stepping down into it. Buck couldn't believe what he saw. "Boss! *Thomas!*"

CHAPTER 8

With the help of his father, Samuel Smith now had a bona fide law office. It wasn't fancy at all, just a desk and two chairs, which suited him just fine. The office was across the street from the mercantile and down a few doors toward the school. Samuel even polished the windows and swept the floors himself. He was hauling his law books in when Luke Bromont showed up to help, possibly hoping to earn a little money. Samuel had heard about how Emma had cooked for the cowboys and how Luke had earned cash for helping. The attorney suspected the boy had acquired a taste for working for pay, but he didn't mind. He was glad for the help and set Luke to dusting the shelves and arranging the books in alphabetical order.

Samuel didn't intend or want to set up a booming law practice. He just needed a place for his things to be and to hold conferences with clients on occasion. It was actually the situation with the Tarrant County records that had provoked him into finding an office.

Birdville was a neighboring community and the county seat; all of the county records had been kept there. But back in the summer, the records were stolen and hidden in a secret location somewhere in Fort Worth.

He thought about the small feud that had broken out over the ownership of the records. and which town would prevail. A town was bound to grow if it was the county seat, and the citizens of Fort Worth were as anxious to be that as Birdville was to regain its position. Gunfire had been exchanged, so Tex and his Rangers had decided to hang around for the time being.

The law was that the records had to be in a public location, but it wasn't safe to have that location generally known. If it were, then the papers would be vulnerable to theft. Tempers would continue to flare up and someone could be hurt or killed. Tex—as a Texas Ranger—and Samuel were the authorities over the records awaiting the state to make its decision concerning the possession law. It could take a lengthy amount of time for the whole thing to be settled.

Samuel stood at the window looking out. He had a nice view of Fort Worth. After Major Ripply and his men had left, the abandoned fort buildings went up for grabs. Now the abandoned fort had a new beginning as a town. Though it didn't yet have a courthouse, it was shaping up with a school, church, livery, general store, and now his law office. He guessed that he would need to hang a shingle over the door.

Jeremiah Longmont stopped his wagon in front of the mercantile to drop off his wife, Katie, and their three children. Samuel admired Jeremiah and the life he had, and somewhat wistfully watched as his friend helped each child out of the wagon safely. Jeremiah kept the little blonde girl in his arms and walked to the boards of the sidewalk before he let her down. Samuel could see them talking and smiling at each other. The little girl gave a hop of excitement over the words from her papa. Her pudgy arm went around his neck and she kissed him. Jeremiah gave a kiss to his daughter and his wife as she went up the steps. He then bounded to his wagon and drove straight to Samuel's office.

It was clear to Samuel why Jeremiah Longmont made a great family man, and he walked out to see him.

"Greetings," Jeremiah said as he pulled the brake on his wagon.

"Hello," Samuel returned and put his hand out to welcome him.

"Just wanted to stop by and let you know we're all set for the hunt. With the full moon on Friday, it should be a great time. I dropped Katie off at the store. She is excited to get the women and children organized for the night."

"That's perfect, Jeremiah! Thanks a lot," Samuel expressed with gratitude. "When my associates arrive, we will be ready for the wolf hunt."

﹡   ﹡   ﹡

As Katie Longmont held the door open for her three children to enter the mercantile, the tinkling of the bell floated to Liz, who was feeling better today. She was still unsure as to whether or not she was pregnant and had decided not to worry Thomas until she had certain news for him. She pictured him galloping around his ranch after his herds, singing with the cowboys under the starry skies, working hard under the open air in fulfillment of his dream, more hale and alive than ever.

"Katie, good to see you." Liz smiled and approached her friend. She slid her pencil in her thick braid and bent down to the children. "Would you like a gumdrop while your mother and I visit?"

Blonde curls bounced on all three as they nodded. Daisy, the oldest, led the other two to the table with a checkerboard. Liz passed out the gumdrops and turned back to Katie.

"We met Thomas on the road the other day with his herd and a new bunch of cowboys." The Longmonts' spread was between Thomas's ranch and Fort Worth.

"Yes, he has gone to the ranch land. He is so pleased. He didn't expect to get it all started so soon." Liz looked for the wooden stool so that she could rest a moment. "I'm not sure when he will return."

"He will be back before you know it. I can see that you're missing him. I'll have Jeremiah keep an eye on the new cowboys." Katie set some quilting thread on the counter. "I need one-half yard of muslin, too."

Liz stood to measure it. "When will we have our next quilting? I need to have a good visit and catch up with everyone. The days have just been spinning here."

"That's what I want to talk to you about."

Katie spoke with excitement as she told Liz about the plans. "Samuel has lawyer friends from the city come each year for a wolf hunt. They pay Jeremiah to conduct a hunt on our land and lead the way with the dogs sniffing the wolves out. The women usually have a big dinner for the men at dusk and then we quilt all night. When we hear the dogs coming back about four a.m., we cook up a big breakfast for everyone."

Liz couldn't believe what she heard. "A wolf hunt here? I thought it was only the coyotes that we heard howling."

"Yes," Katie said. "We have several packs along the Trinity."

"Do they really hunt wolves? What do they do with them?"

"Wolf meat makes great jerky, sausage, and stew," Katie said, "but they don't always go for the kill. It's just the hunt they like."

"Well," Liz said with the last snip of her scissors on the muslin, "I guess we are in for a night of festivities." Liz would look forward to the gathering of friends but wasn't sure about hunting for the thrill of it. City people had a strange way of looking at things.

"I'll see you Friday at Anna's then." Katie handed her a list of things to bring and winked, teasing, "It's a full moon you know; anything can happen."

"Oh, Katie, stop trying to scare me," Liz returned with a smile. "I'll get the news to the others. They will be excited for a break and a good visit. How many quilt racks do we need?"

"It's all in the note there. Anna can fill you in if you have any questions." Katie beckoned to her children just as Jeremiah pulled up with his wagon.

"See you then," the women sang in unison.

※　　※　　※

Anna Parker was standing with her brother, Samuel, in front of his law office as the Longmonts rode over the hill at the edge of town. She had a beautiful quilt folded over her arm that their late mother had made for Samuel. Made of brown and blue triangle scraps surrounding a muslin diamond center, it was called Bachelor's Puzzle. The long triangle unit was a trademark in all of her mother's quilts.

"Mother wanted you to have this when you set up housekeeping." Anna smiled. "Do you need the help of a woman's touch in your place upstairs?"

"Thanks, sis, but I'm all good. The quilt was the last thing I needed."

"You know you're always welcome at mealtime."

"Yeah, thanks, little sis."

Samuel may have been talking to his sister, but his eyes were elsewhere. Anna followed them to see what caught his attention and was not surprised to see Abby walking across the road. She cleared her throat and asked, "Have you been eating with Papa some? I worry about you two old bachelors."

"Don't worry, we're eating just fine. Say, do you happen to know if Abby has been to the Grahams' place yet?"

"She asked me about it, but I doubt she has been. She doesn't know the way."

"Doesn't school start Monday?"

"Yes."

"I better go check it out. See you later, sis."

Holding the bulky quilt, Anna watched, bemused, as her brother hustled to the schoolyard.

※　※　※

Buck starting running down into the ravine toward his boss and friend, boots skidding on the sloping land. He checked himself as his eyes caught a glimpse of the largest rattlesnake he had ever seen lying motionless near Thomas.

He knew the snake might strike back if approached and startled, so he proceeded with great care, intent on reaching Thomas as soon as possible. A breath of relief escaped as he realized the creature was dead. But was Thomas—?

Carefully approaching and looking around in case the dead snake had a comrade close by, he made his way to Thomas and gently nudged him. He said softly, "Thomas? Can you hear me?"

Thomas moaned and held his head.

So he was alive.

"Can you move your feet?"

Thomas could.

"Wiggle your fingers."

Thomas moaned again but to Buck's relief was able to do as he asked. Buck gingerly examined Thomas's neck and back. His ripped clothing was bloody, he had a lump on his head, and he would probably develop a colorful eye later in the day. "What happened? Can you tell me?"

"I'm fine," Thomas mumbled, assuring him. He tried to rise but fell back. "The horse threw me after the snake scared him. I flew off and hit the dirt wall as well as a few branches along the way."

"I assume no snake bites?" Buck knew he needed to get him back to camp. He whistled again so Flip and Easy could find them, and they quickly appeared. The three helped him up the ravine, but Buck looked back.

"Thomas, do you want that rattlesnake hide? Even with a bullet in it, it makes a great trophy."

Thomas didn't open his eyes but nodded and managed a grin. "Sure."

※　※　※

Abby hadn't known Samuel was around and now he was in step with her.

"Hello, Miss Wilkes." Samuel greeted her pleasantly, wanting to broach the subject of the visit to Peter Graham's without sounding interfering.

"Hello, Mr. Smith," she said as she smiled at him.

Samuel knew she expected him to tease her a little, since he usually did. Now he hoped the matter on his mind would just come around in the conversation casually.

"Are you on your way to Anna's? She is actually over at my new place above the law office."

Abby stopped. "You have moved your personal belongings? I wasn't aware you were going to live there too."

"Can't live with my father forever. Guess it's time I got out on my own." Samuel smiled as he added, "I really did need an office, especially in light of the situation about the county seat. Living above it just makes good sense. Anna's putting a woman's touch, as she calls it, on the place."

"I was looking for Anna, but if she's busy I guess I can find her later."

Samuel noticed her worried look. His aim was to get her to accept his help. He decided to get right to the point.

"Miss Wilkes." He spoke formally. "I'm aware that you intend to go to Peter Graham's home and I understand you want to do it today. Anna spoke with Parker about it and he in turn spoke with me. Abby, it just isn't safe for the two of you to go alone."

Abby stopped and turned to Samuel. She started to protest but Samuel put his hand up in a mannerly way to stop her. He kept his hand up as he spoke.

"Miss Wilkes, I promise that I will be on my best behavior. I can get the wagon and drive you out at any time. It will be 'all official.' You will be content to make this home visit and your school elders will be satisfied that you are safe. Mr. Graham is unstable, but we do want that boy in school."

Samuel did a fine job presenting his case to Abby, almost as though he were in a courtroom and hoped she would see the point.

"Well, you make a good argument, Mr. Smith. I wouldn't want to put Anna in any danger on my account." She paused. "Or have Pastor Parker upset over any of it." Abby laid one finger across her lips, thinking seriously. "Mr. Smith, do you pledge to be on your best behavior?"

She was so intent. Samuel knew if he smiled or smirked that the deal was off. His motive was to help her, but spending an afternoon with her would be an added bonus.

"Yes, ma'am, I promise," Samuel said with all the dignity he could muster, and he even managed to hold back his smile.

"When can you be ready?" she asked. She caught the twinkle in his eye. Samuel almost jumped with joy, but instead he put his energy into hustling to the livery.

"Right away, Miss Wilkes. I'll be right back with the wagon."

Abby couldn't help smiling as she watched Samuel take off. He returned with his wagon so quickly that she barely had time to prepare her thoughts for the meeting with Peter's father.

As Abby bounced around in the wagon, she found it hard to carry on even light conversation with Samuel. He spent most of his words on the team of horses, coaxing them along.

After driving on a rough road for a length of time, Samuel said, "We're almost there; it's just around that bend of trees."

Samuel and Abby pulled up in front of the Grahams' place. A path from the road to the broken-down cabin was barely visible, hidden by the late summer weeds that were so tall they almost reached Abby's waist. Chickens wandered around the unkempt grounds, easily catching their meal of plentiful bugs that were flying or hopping in every direction. Abby had never seen chickens in such an excited state of pecking and chasing before.

The wagon stopped and Samuel started to pull the brake, but was hesitant because of what he saw. Maybe the father and son had gone away.

Abby sat in disbelief. After a moment, she gathered her courage and her skirt to climb down from the wagon. Samuel realized she intended to go to the door and put a hand on her arm to stop her.

"Abby, wait here and let me check it out first."

He secured the brake on the wagon and hopped down; chickens clucked and scattered in all directions.

"Hellooooo . . . Anyone home?" Samuel called out, swatting flies and gnats as he went.

He reached the door, which was slightly open. It was dark inside and Samuel couldn't see well. Something made a sound and an old dog sauntered over to the door where he stood. His ribs were showing but his tail had a good wag to it.

"Hey old guy, you alone?" Samuel asked and patted the dog. Samuel kept his head up, still looking around. His eyes were adjusting to the dark now. The inside of the cabin was worse than the outside and it smelled sour and musty.

"Samuel," Abby called out in a choked voice.

He turned to see Abby in the wagon with old man Graham holding her at gunpoint.

"You two lookin' for somethin'?" he asked, and his voice was gruff.

Mr. Graham looked and smelled like his homestead.

"Howdy, Mr. Graham. Remember me? I'm Samuel Smith from the fort. This is Miss Abigail Wilkes, our new schoolteacher." Samuel walked slowly to the wagon, the dog following hopefully. "School starts on Monday. We just came out to invite Peter to her classroom."

"Humph," he snorted and kept the gun on Abby. "What fer?"

"Every boy needs learnin'," Samuel said mildly. "Won't hurt him none. He'd be back home again in time for, uh, chores." Samuel kept his eyes on the man not wanting his tone to express his observation that few chores seemed to get done at this place.

Mr. Graham shifted his eyes away from the lawyer. Then he said, "You kin ask the boy." He used his rifle to motion toward the river. "He's went down to the water."

Abby looked at the poor appearance of the father.

"Do you mind if we go down that way?" Samuel asked, now climbing into the wagon and releasing the brake. He gave the horses a slap and started to move out as quickly as he could without disturbing the disheveled man any further.

Abby didn't say a word as they moved closer to the river looking for Peter. She had heard about children in homes that lacked a woman's care, but this was more than she could believe. Her father's slaves lived far above what she had just seen.

Samuel was looking for Peter and trying to watch the path as he drove the wagon. There really wasn't a road at this point. He glanced over at Abby on occasion and was concerned about what she was thinking. He knew this was a home visit the women couldn't have done alone. He heard some voices and stopped the wagon under the shade of some big Texas oaks.

"Abby, it sounds like we found someone. We will have to leave the wagon here and walk the rest of the way."

Samuel jumped out of the wagon and helped Abby down. Dried prairie grass covered the earth, making the surface level for Abby to follow Samuel and move across the ground. Still, he gallantly took her hand and led her to the spot where they heard some boys swimming.

When they finally reached the swimming hole, Abby was surprised by what she saw.

The banks of the Trinity River were steep where she stood. The river could have been much higher but the water still looked deep. A primitive wooden bridge that she would never have stepped foot on hung over the water. At the top of the bridge were several men and six or so half-grown boys. In fact, she was sure these young men were her students. She squinted into the sun and picked out Luke, Nate Turner, and Thayer Tate. As she looked the men over, she saw Jackson dive off the bridge and go straight down into the deep water.

"Was that Jackson?" She gasped and turned to Samuel, wondering if he was as astonished as she was. She looked down to see Jackson at the top of the water hollering for all he was worth.

"I got one! I got one!" he yelled out over gulps of air and splashing water. Jackson swam with one arm while the other arm wrestled with the big catfish as he swam to the rocky edge under the bridge.

Everyone climbed down to help Jackson with the massive fish and congratulated him. Abby suspected the fish would grow as the story of the catch was retold.

"Samuel, what is going on?"

Samuel stood by Abby, watching the action with a huge grin on his face. He was wishing he could go join in on the fun. It had been awhile since he had jumped from the bridge and caught a fish with his bare hands. He could feel the rush of excitement go through him. Samuel waved his arms at the group on the bridge and yelled out a whoop of congratulations to his friends.

"Samuel," Abby said again. "Did you know about this? Is this what Luke was telling me about?"

"Yeah," Samuel said, not looking at Abby.

He was trying to find a way to lead Abby down the steep dirt and rock path to the men. He thought he found a way and took Abby's hand to lead her down.

"Samuel, what are you doing?"

"Let's get closer. I think we can get down this way." Samuel pulled her with him as he pursued his idea.

"I can't go down there! Samuel, those men aren't fully clothed!"

She pulled back on his hand. He stopped and looked at Abby and then to the men scattered around on the bridge, on the rocky shore, and in the water.

"Well, I guess not." He smiled and his eyes got that teasing twinkle. He started to unbutton the top button on his shirt and said, "*We* are a little overdressed, aren't we?"

"You're not serious, are you?" Abby protested. "You promised me you would be on your best behavior!"

Samuel checked his smirk and looked Abby in the eye. "You're right, Miss Wilkes, a promise is a promise. We are here to find your student."

Now that Samuel had turned around to talk with Abby, he saw Peter Graham sitting on a log watching the activity at the bridge.

"I think we found him," he said and motioned over to the boy in the shade of the tree.

Abby turned to see. Before her was a rumpled looking boy. His hair was cut unevenly and his tattered clothing was too small. He looked over at them and quietly looked back at the swimmers.

Before Samuel could say anything else, Abby was on her way over to Peter.

Samuel looked back down at the water and then back to Abby. "I'll give you some time alone," he said and started down the steep incline to the river. He dug the heels of his boots into the banks to keep his balance as he walked and slid to the water's edge.

"Hello, Peter," Abby said gently. "I'm Miss Wilkes. I'm the new schoolteacher. Do you mind if I sit with you awhile?"

Peter scooted over a little on the log. A small smile of acknowledgment brightened his lonely face.

"Why aren't you joining in on the fun with the other boys?"

Peter shrugged his shoulders and was quiet.

Abby now watched the divers and saw Luke jump up in the air. He twisted his body and did a double flip before he hit the water with a big splash. The crowd whooped. Jackson was now at the water's edge and stood in the shade of the bridge. She could see him motion up to where she sat with Peter, and a few of the men waved.

Good heavens, Abby thought, have they no shame? She briefly held a hand up in a wave.

"Would you like to be swimming with the other boys?" she asked again.

"I don't know how in that deep water. Pa never let me get in there at the bridge. Said they were crazy."

Abby smiled and laughed. "Your father may have had more sense than those men at the bridge. If you would like, they can teach you to swim and then you could join in the fun." Splashing and hollering was heard again as two more dove in from the highest point on the wooden bridge.

"Peter, I talked with your father." Abby paused. "He said I should ask you if you would like to be in my classroom."

Peter looked at Abby like she had three eyes. He slowly answered her with his eyes racing back and forth on her eyes. "You want me? I ain't had no schoolin'."

Abby's voice was soft and she smiled at him.

"That's why we go to school—to learn. I don't mind starting at the beginning with you. You look mighty smart to me. I think you will pick up the learning pretty quickly." Her hand was on his shoulder, already sending confidence and encouragement to her student.

Suddenly, the atmosphere changed at the water, the excitement turning to panic. She didn't know what the commotion was all about but instantly started looking for the faces she knew. She found Luke, Nate, and Thayer. Samuel was still on the bank. He was pointing and shouting to Jackson. Jackson dove from the top of the bridge and went sharply into the water. Every eye was on the ripple where he entered. It seemed like minutes went by. Voices quieted.

Abby stood to see if she could see what the problem was. A young boy stood at the bridge with a frightened look.

"Did he get my pa? Did he get my pa?"

No one answered. Everyone still looked at the water, their eyes searching back and forth. Nate pointed to some bubbles now at the surface in the middle of the river.

With an explosion, Jackson surfaced with Leon's pa hoisted over his shoulder pulling him to the shore. Jackson's powerful arm sliced through the water and he was at the rocks quickly. Samuel helped pull Mr. DeJarnette's unmoving body from the water. Blood was seeping from his leg and from the back of his head.

As Jackson was climbing up the rocks, he yelled out to Samuel, "Turn him over, push on his back!"

Samuel flipped Mr. DeJarnette over to his stomach. He was on a grassy area now. Samuel placed one leg over the body and started to push on the back of the man. Water bubbled from his lungs and spewed from his mouth. Samuel pushed again. Jackson was now there and he had someone's shirt. He ripped it in two, used one section on Mr. DeJarnette's head, and wrapped the bleeding leg with the other.

"Do it again," Jackson ordered Samuel and he pushed on the man's back again. Mr. DeJarnette sputtered and coughed, but didn't move. "Do it again," Jackson said. Samuel continued to press rhythmically.

They rolled him on his side as he coughed again, water still coming from his lungs. Mr. DeJarnette's eyes rolled open. He tried to focus and talk but fell unconscious. Jackson put his hand to Mr. DeJarnette's mouth. He could feel air. He placed his hand over the man's heart. It was beating.

"I've got a wagon, Jackson. Let's put him in the wagon and get him to the Parkers. Careful, now." Samuel glanced at Leon and kept his voice low. "We don't know if anything's broken."

"Is my pa gonna live?" Leon asked, standing close with water still dripping from him. He tried to sound brave, but his voice quavered.

"He's alive and his heart feels strong," Jackson said as he prepared to help lift him gently into the wagon.

Abby and Peter stood out of the way watching the men work.

"Guess I don't care much about that learnin' to swim," Peter re-marked with wide eyes.

"Oh, Peter," Abby said. She ruffled his hair and grabbed his hand as they hurried to the wagon.

Samuel finished settling Mr. DeJarnette in the back of the buck-board and turned to look for Abby. She had just about reached him with Peter in tow. She had one hand on her skirt holding it up a little and the other firmly gripped her student.

"Guess you caught what you were looking for," Samuel said, trying to reassure Abby.

CHAPTER 9

When Bet saw the men riding back to camp and Thomas clearly hurt, she grabbed rags and towels and ran quickly out to meet them.

"Get him on a cot," she said, forgetting to deepen her voice. She and Buck met each other's eyes as, stricken, she realized her mistake. She quickly recovered and added, low, "Hurry it up, now!"

Pulling off her ever-present gloves, she expertly tended to her boss's wounds. He would be fine.

For the next couple of days, Bet cared for Thomas, cheered by his quick recuperation, but insistent that he not go back to his routine too quickly. Head wounds could be difficult, she reminded him. She joined in with the rest of the ranchers teasing him about his black-and-purple eye, though concerned that some of them were guessing her secret. Had Buck noticed her voice?

Buck had ridden out to the ravine and recovered the snake. The creature was skinned and its shiny patterned scales were stretched out drying in the full sun and the rattles were sewn to Thomas's hat band. He refused Easy's offer to ride out to town and tell Liz what had happened. No point in fretting her. She'd know soon enough, and maybe he'd present her with a snakeskin belt.

Bet cooked up the snake meat for the hungry cowhands and earned rave reviews. Thomas had not eaten much over the last couple of days and was finally ready for some solid food. Bet didn't fuss over him but gave him salve and bandages for his cuts and scrapes; only one cut was deep enough to worry about and give him some trouble.

Thomas watched Bet while he was laid up in camp and had also come to the conclusion that his cook was a female. The only time she had her gloves off, besides when she was doctoring him that first day, was when she stitched the rattles onto his hat. Even though he wasn't close he could tell they were dainty and feminine. Thomas rolled the matter over in his head for days and finally decided to bring it up to her. Camp was quiet, so now was as good a time as any.

Bet came over with a fresh pot of coffee and Thomas asked her to stay a minute. Her custom was to do what was needed, then quickly return to the chuck wagon, never lingering long or saying much more than what was necessary. Now at Thomas's request she remained, still standing but looking apprehensive.

"Everything good for you, boss?" Bet asked as the breeze blew her locks over her eyes. A gloved hand moved them slightly as Thomas saw a frightened look for just a moment as she glanced toward the chuck wagon. Thomas thought she wanted to scoot to safety under the wagon wheels and hide. She wasn't very old—maybe even younger than Emma. He decided to get straight to the point and talk to her about her disguise.

"Bet, is there anything you would like to tell me?"

She hesitated. Her mouth moved, but nothing came out. She glanced longingly at the chuck wagon again.

"It's okay. Sit on this log." Thomas tried to calm her, but she seemed to feel cornered. Her feet shuffled.

"Are you happy with me, sir? I'm sorry if I've messed up. Just tell me, I'll do better." She almost begged.

"Bet," Thomas said. He had her attention and watched as she blinked and looked him square in the face, knowing her jig was up. "I know you're a woman. We all know. Your secret is safe with us. Do you want to tell me what you are hiding from or running from?" She hesitated again. "You are as safe here as any one of the other workers. No one is going to give you up. Are you in trouble? Maybe with the law?"

Bet took her hat off and ran her hands through her short, sun-tinted, glossy locks. "I guess I should have known you'd figure it out," she said as she sat down on the log. She relaxed a moment and continued in her own voice, no longer attempting to sound like a baritone. "Sir, my name is Bethany. I come from south Texas, but please don't send me back down there."

"How old are you, Bethany? Where is your family?"

"I'm almost seventeen, sir. My mother and sisters were killed in an Indian raid. My pa thought I would be safer away, so he sent me to his brother's house to help out with his family." She had a sad but panicky look about her as she mentioned her uncle.

"And you left them? Are they looking for you?"

"I think for a while they did, but I'm not sure now."

"What happened when you were there? Why did you leave?" She looked down after a glance at Thomas, who asked gently, "Why are you so afraid?"

"My uncle," she stammered. "He—he took advantage of me in the barn when I was tending the horses. I became . . . with child." Bet paused and swallowed. "And my aunt said it was my fault he did that. She beat me. A lot. And my baby was born, but it was too early and she couldn't survive." Her eyes filled with tears. "She was so sweet and so, so tiny."

As Thomas watched her give this sad account, he saw not someone swaggering and trying to fit in with a crowd of cowboys, but a young girl who had seen more hardship than was fair for her years.

She continued, "And after my baby died, I stole one of the horses and ran away. I don't care that I stole his horse. I had to get away."

She looked up at Thomas with sad eyes. Silent tears fell as she waited for the next turn of events to tumble down into her young life. Had she been one of the Mailly women, Thomas would have reached out to comfort her, but thought it was best now that he keep his distance. She was as skittish as a kitten in a thunderstorm.

"Bet, I'm sorry to hear you lost your mother and your sisters in such a horrible way. I'm glad you and your father were spared. And I'm sorry your baby died."

Bethany tried to curb her sniffles as Thomas went on. "I'm so sorry your uncle had his way with you. It wasn't right. It was not your fault that he did that. It was his fault. He is not a good man, and your aunt is not someone you need to be around." He paused, letting his words sink in. "Do you want to stay on here as our cook? We are good men. No one will misuse you here. You have my word. We'd like you to stay."

She nodded and wiped the tears from her cheeks. She straightened her shoulders, and Thomas saw a gleam of hope in her eyes.

"We—all of us here at the Rolling M Ranch—are your family now and we will protect you. If you want to keep dressing as a man, that is okay with us. We will keep your secret from anyone who might come around asking."

Bet stood and dried her last tear. Thomas stood too. "Bethany, do you know the Lord and His saving powers?"

She nodded and stared at her boss.

"Good, then. You are a daughter of the King and He washed you white as snow, made you new again. You have no reason to feel ashamed or at fault. You hear me? You understand?"

"Yes, sir," she said, mulling over what he said.

"Anytime you feel that way, think on that. Okay?"

She nodded her head again and stooped to pick up the coffeepot. She started to walk away, then turned and spoke with resolve. "Yessir. Thank you, boss. You remind me of my pa." She took another step and stopped to turn. "And that's good."

Thomas smiled and asked, "Do you want to try and find him?"

"I'll think on it some," she said and walked to her refuge of the chuck wagon.

Thomas thought she had a bit of a bounce in her step as she walked away.

※　※　※

Megan and Emma cooked a nice supper with the catfish Luke had caught that morning. Fresh sliced tomatoes from the garden, corn bread, and battered okra finished out the meal. Emma had made another batch of peach cobbler since they were shorted earlier in the week. Liz, Luke, and Abby were regulars at most meals, but they were never sure who else would also stumble in to eat with them. Megan had decided to emulate Anna Parker, who said she never knew who the Lord would send to share her table, and typically prepared extra. Megan admired that the Parkers' home was always open to guests. The Rangers were good friends and usually dropped by when they were in town, as well as Samuel. These men were never strangers at their table.

Emma set out fresh butter. The horse she was doctoring was responding well to her attention and would be ready to ride again in a few days. Since Thomas and the cowboys could be back from the ranch by the weekend, she needed to be prepared to buy the horse or let it go.

"Do you think any of the Rangers will show up for supper?" Megan asked. She hadn't seen the youngest Ranger, Colt, in a good while but knew he wasn't far away if Tex and Jackson were still around. She had learned to like Colt, even with his long hair and smart mouth. With the county records still being fussed about and peaceable relations between the towns in jeopardy, she figured he was in Birdville keeping an eye on the good citizens and would ride in anytime. She was glad Jackson stayed in town. Megan enjoyed visiting with him. He was easy to talk with, he smelled good, and he was mannerly besides.

"Do you know when Abby will return?" Megan asked Emma, who was just opening the oven door to slide the cobbler inside.

"No, but Liz didn't think she would be late. Samuel stopped in the store to tell Liz he was taking Abby out in a wagon to the Graham place."

"I'm sure she was happy with that." Emma giggled. "The first time he made her ride a horse and she was in her nice skirt."

Emma liked Samuel and enjoyed watching him ruffle her sister's feathers. It was good for her sometimes overly proper sister to be teased. Samuel could usually get away with it when she couldn't.

"She left that day mad as a wet cat." Emma laughed at the memory. She placed the towels she had used to open the hot oven door on the table. She pulled out a chair and sat down for a moment.

"Yes," Megan said and looked over to her cousin, "but she came home plenty cheerful after her last outing with Mr. Smith."

Emma's expression was quizzical as she said, "Do you think he's sweet on her?"

"Samuel and Abby?" Megan repeated. "How did I miss that one?" That was like a rooster getting a surprise sunrise. "Well, I never thought on that. Maybe so; they would make a nice couple." She stopped flipping the catfish in the hot skillet. It sizzled and popped, making its announcement as well as any dinner bell.

Luke made a thundering noise on the porch as he ran through the back door out of breath.

"Mr. DeJarnette," he panted, "in the wagon." He took a breath and gasped out, "Samuel and Miss Abby." He leaned on his knees, "almost dead."

Emma was out the door headed to the main road before Luke could get the rest of the story told.

Megan hurriedly took the skillet from the stove and burned her finger. "Samuel and Abby? Luke, what are you saying? Who is almost dead?" She popped her finger in her mouth to relieve the pain. She stared at him waiting for the answer.

"Jackson—" Luke was still trying to catch his breath.

At the mention of Jackson, Megan's heart leaped. Luke managed to say, "Mr. DeJarnette. Almost drowned. Jackson saved him."

Everyone had gathered at the Parkers' house and they had Mr. DeJarnette carried inside. Anna and Parker were seeing to him while Samuel gave details of the accident. Someone sent for Mrs. Perkins. Jackson sat on the end of the wagon cleaning blood off him. Anna had given him a bucket of fresh water, soap, and some rags.

"Jackson! Jackson!" Megan called as soon as she could see him. "Are you hurt?" She was close enough to see him covered with blood. "Where is it coming from?" Megan had a cloth and was wiping the blood from his chest and shoulders.

"Well, howdy," Jackson said calmly, looking at the young women. He nodded at Megan and Emma and stopped washing. He dropped the cloth in the bucket of water. The water started to turn pink.

"How can you be so calm? Where is all of this coming from?" Megan kept cleaning the blood off the big man. "Jackson, stop grinning and tell me what happened!" she demanded.

Abby came out of Anna's doorway and went to the wagon. She had Leon DeJarnette and Peter Graham with her.

"Jackson doesn't have any of his own blood on him . . . do you?" Abby looked at Jackson.

"So many questions, ladies," Jackson said, enjoying all the female attention. "Thank you for worrying about me so, but it's Mr. DeJarnette, Leon's pa, who was hurt." He looked at the boy with the tearstained face standing with Abby. Jackson quickly realized that Leon was scared to death and worried about his pa and he stopped joking.

"He had a bad knock on his head and hurt his leg, but Miss Anna will have him good as new before we know it, maybe even before Mrs. Perkins turns up." Jackson gave the young man some confidence with his words. Leon sniffled and wiped at a stray tear with the back of his hand.

Emma decided to take the boys and Abby home to finish supper. She knew once the boys were fed and cleaned up she could get the story on what took place with Mr. DeJarnette.

"Abby, would you like to take the boys home and feed them? I'm sure they're famished after all of the swimming. We almost have it ready; it will only take me a minute to get it on the table."

"That sounds wonderful. Gentlemen, let's go to the house." Abby gathered her students and started toward her home with Emma.

"Good heavens! I forgot about the peach cobbler in the oven!" Emma took off running.

"Jackson, tell me what happened," Megan said, after it got quiet again. "Is Mr. DeJarnette going to be all right? With all of this blood," she paused and looked at Jackson, "it looks real bad." Jackson got serious and told Megan what happened at the bridge. The man must have hit his head on some rocks, which accounted for the amount of blood. It was worrying that he hadn't yet regained consciousness, but Jackson had seen such injuries before, and did not believe these were life-threatening or permanent. The man did not have a neck or back injury, of that he was certain. Mr. DeJarnette's leg would have to be in a splint in order to heal cleanly. When he finished, she was more at ease but knew Leon's pa was a lucky man to be alive.

"Jackson, you saved his life," she whispered.

"All in the line of duty, ma'am." Jackson tried to cheer her up.

"We have plenty for supper if you are in the mood for catfish," Megan said. Megan was so small that with him sitting in the wagon bed and her standing, they were face to face.

Megan reached over to pour out the bucket of stained water. She didn't know how close she had come to being kissed by the gentle giant.

"Let's go see about supper," she said as she smiled at him.

"Jackson," she asked as they walked to the house. "What is your full name?"

"Jackson," he replied.

"Jackson what?"

"Why?"

Megan stopped and asked, "Do all men in the West go by one name or is it just the Rangers? Tex. Colt. Jackson." She punctuated each name to prove her point. "Don't any of you have a first and a last name?"

"Ian. It's Ian Jackson."

"Ian," Megan repeated as they walked on to the house for supper. "That's real nice, Jackson."

Luke, Leon, and Peter had just finished washing up. Abby had borrowed one of Luke's shirts for Peter. It was one that he wouldn't be wearing anymore since he had taken a growth spurt. Peter wasn't talking much but Luke and Leon did a fine job of including Peter in the conversation.

"Peter, do you want to learn to dive from the bridge?" Luke asked.

"No," was all Peter said, but it had a ring to it of "are you crazy?"

"We have been swimming there and fishin' there since my pa was a boy and no one ever got hurt. It was just a fluke. I'm sure my pa will do it again once he's on his feet." Leon paused. "If Ma lets him." Someone had sent word to Mrs. DeJarnette, who would surely be invited to spend the night at the Parkers' since her husband shouldn't yet be moved. Leon would bunk with Luke, and one of the men from town would see that Peter Graham got home safely.

Abby and Emma giggled at Leon's honesty.

Emma had saved the cobbler from overbaking and it was perfectly browned on top. It smelled grand. The catfish was steaming hot and arranged appetizingly on a plate in the middle of the table. Emma put more fish in the pan and it sizzled.

"Luke, say grace for us and you boys may start." Abby gave the boys an approving look. She was as happy as she could be mothering her group of students. She poured milk into three tall glasses and set them before the boys.

The two sisters spoke quietly by the stove and flipped the rest of the catfish. Emma listened as Abby gave an account of her day. Emma looked at Peter and Leon and thought they were both lucky boys. She liked them and was glad Luke had made some good friends.

The boys finished quickly and went to the porch where Bear was waiting. Cally, the yellow cat, was sleeping contentedly after her tasty supper of fish tails.

Emma took the plates off the table and reset it just as Megan and Jackson came home.

Abby looked to see how the supply of supper was holding out. "Megan, you and Emma must have been cooking all day," she said.

Jackson's shirt was so torn and tattered it was barely hanging on him with its one remaining sleeve. He planned on adding it to the rag basket. He towered over Megan as they stood together in the doorway.

"Jackson, as soon as you start eating, I'll take your shirt and get it back in wearable condition again. I haven't sewn in weeks with all the canning to be done. I'm anxious to get stitching again. I think I can use my treadle on most of it." She looked at a button that was hanging by a thread.

Luke poked his head in the door. "Ma is eating at Anna's and Mr. DeJarnette is waking up. She's gonna stay and help out for a while." He was gone as quickly as he came.

"Looks like we have leftovers for tomorrow," Emma said. Everyone who was hungry had been fed, and they had arranged for Little Dove to pick up a basket of food for the Parker household.

Abby went to the door to see if Samuel was about. She hadn't gotten to talk with him about Peter or Mr. DeJarnette, or thank him for the wagon.

Jackson sat on the porch with a big bowl of cobbler and rocked. Evening was a good time to think over the day. A cool breeze came through and tried to chill him as he sat in the dark. He could hear the hum of Megan's treadle as she repaired his shirt.

Emma finished cleaning the kitchen. Abby had the boys settled for bed in Luke's room and completed the evening chores. Simultaneously they all appeared on the porch with Jackson.

"What a day," Abby said as she sat in a rocker. "Jackson, you were great, helping Leon's pa like that. Thank you."

He nodded and scooped up more peach cobbler. Emma sat on a bench under the kitchen window and Megan found a seat on the steps of the porch. She could see the beauty of the night sky. It was clear except for the hazy ring around the moon.

"The moon is almost full," Megan said as she looked up to a Texas sky shining with stars. "But see the circle that surrounds it? That means rain is on the way."

Jackson rocked on the porch and looked up at the moon. He could certainly get used to this relaxed feeling. But it was really more than that. He was getting to know this family and he respected them. This little band of women was tough and soft all at the same time. He had never been a part of a real family and thought he could get used to it. A full stomach and a rocking chair on a moonlit night were mighty close to heaven.

Three lovely ladies to share it with didn't hurt any either.

❅   ❅   ❅

For days Liz had been wanting to get some time alone with Megan. She knew something was wrong and she suspected what it was about. Megan had been quiet and just wasn't her usual self. Her sweet spirit that usually brought happiness and excitement to a room had been missing. Liz had been watching her and knew that she wasn't concentrating on her work as there had been no activity at her table for at least twenty minutes.

Megan looked up from the table at the mercantile where she had been deep in thought. She dropped her pencil and gave a look of confusion and despair. Tears welled up in her bluish-green eyes.

"I don't want to, I can't do it," she sighed and leaned her cheek on her hand.

Liz came over to the table ready to talk it out with her baby sister.

"Tell me what you are thinking about; I know something has bothered you for days. When we voice our worries the way to go becomes more clear." She pulled the chair away from the small table and set it across from her sister.

Megan slumped her shoulders and sighed again. "It's Jackson."

"What about Jackson?"

"I—I think I might love him." She choked back a sob. "I've tried to push the feeling away but it just won't go away."

Liz suppressed her smile; it was just as she thought. Her sister was in love again, but this time Liz really liked the man. She waited for her sister to dab at the tears and say more. She knew talking about what was on her mind would be good for Megan. And of course, a prayer never hurt, so Liz prayed silently for her sister.

Megan began again, "After Matthew I never wanted a man in my life. I never understood how we could be so perfect for each other and so in love and he would do what he did to me, just toss me away like an old pair of socks." She stumbled over her words, the memory of those dark days still hurtful. "I mean, how could he choose his mother over me? Even the two family businesses were a perfect match but after she met me she made Matthew leave me." Megan's sobs threatened to return and she swiped at a few tears impatiently.

Liz remembered the event as if it were yesterday. The heartbreak her sister had endured was almost more than she could bear. Her grandfather was so upset with Matthew that he cancelled all of the timber mill contracts with the Coldwell family and never sold to them again. He told Matthew to never come back even if he changed his mind and broke loose of the apron strings his mother held so tightly.

Mrs. Coldwell was as disapproving of Megan's free-spirited personality as she was on the hold the young woman had on her son's heart. Not wanting to lose Matthew to Megan, she not so subtly forbade the relationship to go any further.

Liz reasoned with the sad Megan. "You weren't a limp, mealy-mouthed woman that would cower to a mother-in-law. She saw you as a threat."

"But how could Matthew leave me if he loved me like he said? I've never understood that. Maybe he didn't love me at all." She gulped at the realization.

"Some men aren't—well, some don't learn how to be a man. To love and respect their mother but turn to a wife after they marry is foreign. Some mothers only raise boys and don't know how to raise men. To train any child, give your life for them, and then be willing to release them to become adults is more than they can do. It is hard." Liz spoke with first-hand knowledge. "I've always told myself with Luke that I am raising a man, not training a boy. A mother can't be selfish."

Liz could see that Megan was listening. Liz explained that it is hard to nurture a child from birth and then see him grow up and away from his mother, but that's what children are supposed to do. Megan was calming down.

"Grandpa did raise us to be strong willed and independent, but not everyone admires that trait of the Mailly women," Liz observed. "But can't you see that we are better for it as long as we know how to check ourselves when necessary?" Liz mused about how she often needed to think first and speak second with Thomas. It wasn't easy. She continued, "We think for ourselves and make sound decisions. So you are able to make a good decision about this, Megan." Liz gave Megan's self-confidence a boost. "So what worries you the most over this emotion with Jackson?"

"I have been thinking about that. First, just the fact of loving and not getting it in return. That he would leave me like Matthew."

"Well, I don't think that would happen. I don't see Jackson with that character trait. He is a man not tied to anything except his work."

"That's another problem," Megan stated with emphasis. "He is a lawman through and through. Do I want a husband who earns a living by the gun on his hip? Will we always be looking over our shoulder for the trouble that comes looking for him? He is gone for days at a time. I would never know where he was or if he was coming back. Even if he chooses to leave the Rangers, some bandit with a chip on his shoulder and with revenge to carry out could come along."

Megan had certainly been thinking this out, Liz reasoned, and told her so.

Megan nodded and bit the side of her lip, a mannerism she shared with her sister.

Liz thought a moment before she asked, "Has Jackson told you that he is interested in you? I know he spends a lot of time with our family, but that doesn't mean he is ready to settle down with a wife and children. It could just be the readily available food," she cautioned with a laugh.

"No, and that is another thing." Megan sighed again. "Usually a man who spends that much time with me or our family would have given a sign or talked with me about a courtship. Jackson has never given a hint in any direction one way or another. He could be silently pining away for Abby or Emma and I could end up like Thomas, watching someone I'm close to marry the man I love."

Liz hadn't thought about that. All of the women could be married off in a short time. She decided to lighten the mood. "Maybe that is what Grandpa wanted when he sent us all west so quickly: to marry. I guess we scared off all the gentlemen in the South. The men of the West are not afraid of our spunk or attitude. It is a required trait here."

Megan started to become herself again, Liz noticed. Visiting with her sister always cleared her head and this time hopefully her heart too. "Anyway, there is no mother or family to get in the way this time."

Liz smiled. "That can be a blessing, but it would be sad to not have a family and to be on your own in the world."

Megan grabbed her sister's hand and smiled, "Yes, I can't even think about not having you."

Liz squeezed back. "Is there anything else that bothers you about falling in love with Jackson?"

"Do I allow my heart to go on loving this man? Do I think about his employment as a hindrance? And if I do continue, do I tell him or wait for Jackson to make the first move?"

Liz looked at her sister. "Well, only you can decide, Megan, but I will say that it was better to have loved Caleb, even though he was lost to me too soon, than never to have had him at all. Nothing on this earth is promised for tomorrow."

Megan listened to what Liz was saying, still a little tearfully, but looking more confident.

"Pray about clarity with Jackson and if you decide to let your heart go, ask God to nudge Jackson in that direction. It is always good for the man to think it is his decision. Just continue being your sweet, optimistic self. You will be a wonderful wife and I look forward to sharing that part of your life with you. I will also pray for you and Jackson to know what is best for you and for God to bless you and care for you no matter what happens."

At this Megan smiled, hugged her sister goodbye, and left out the back door.

Chapter 10

Liz woke on that Friday morning to a cloudy day. The sun tried occasionally to peek out and then another thunderhead would roll in and cover the sky. Rain had fallen several times during the night in short bursts. She had gotten used to sleeping with Thomas and shivered as she searched for the warmth of his body. This was the first cool night and Liz hadn't lit the stove or placed a quilt on the bed before going to sleep. She was just too tired to get up in the darkness and throw on an extra cover. Instead, she pulled her legs up in her gown and tucked it in at her feet. She folded her arms close to her chest and tried to drift off. Sleep would not visit her again that night as she lay awake thinking.

She was happy living above the mercantile with Thomas, though their cozy home just consisted of a small bedroom with enough room for a table and a stove for heating. Her family lived just outside their back door in a house that had two bedrooms, a parlor, and big kitchen with a table that they could all sit around. The Lukes and Thomas had built on a third bedroom for young Luke and enlarged the back porch. It now extended all the way to the bathhouse.

Rain spattered at the windows again and Liz shivered as her feet hit the floor. She quickly got out of bed, smoothed some loose hair back into her braid, and ran for the quilt that lay carefully on the chair, wrapping it around her shoulders. This was the quilt Thomas had given her as a gift. It had colorful circles and she fondly recalled the heartfelt gesture

Thomas had made. He was a giving, considerate man with the backbone to temper Liz's strong will on occasion. Previously, her grandfather was the only man Liz had ever acceded to. She did have a stubborn streak that she had to work on more often than she cared to admit. Thomas was loving but quick to defend his way when necessary, something he had made clear early in their relationship. The quilt had started out as a gift and become an ultimatum.

She remembered it was a cloudy morning like this that she almost lost Thomas. She quickly pushed forward in her memory to the point that all had worked out and they were now married. Very happily.

Liz missed her husband. She didn't know how long he would be gone. She looked out the window and gazed over the countryside as though she could see her man across the miles.

Liz prayed, "Lord, keep Thomas safe and warm in this rain. Help him with the new responsibilities of the ranch and the construction of barns and corrals. Bring him back to me soon."

Liz felt a wave of dizziness and nausea come over her as she hurried to a little chamber pot. She hadn't eaten much the day before and had nothing in her stomach now. Her stomach was revolting with emptiness and her head hurt. She found a small cloth, poured some water into it, and cooled her flushed face. She pulled the quilt over her shoulders and rested in the chair by the front window. Her head leaned against the glass. She placed her hand over her stomach. It hurt from the heaving of a few moments ago.

"What is wrong with me?" she whispered. "Am I sick? Or am I going to have a baby?"

She thought back to the doctor telling her that Luke would be her only child. He didn't know why. He said God made the rules, he didn't. Liz had adjusted to the fact.

So much had happened in the last eighteen months, she reflected. Her first husband, Caleb, had died at the timber mill in a logging accident and they never found his body. Her grandfather, predicting that the turmoil in the country would erupt in a civil war, sold their family land

and business, and moved them all west. In the move, they were in a tornado, stranded from all the male help and forced to go west alone, where they encountered Indians and searched for the Texas fort they would call home. After they got to Fort Worth, she started the mercantile and freight business, where she was robbed and her grandfather murdered. She and Thomas had married. Now Thomas was far away building the ranch that he and her grandfather had wanted, planned, and dreamed about.

No wonder she was tired and emotionally drained. She turned to her God as she always did, especially when her strength was waning.

"Lord, I need You now and always. Strengthen me, mind, body, and spirit. Heal me in all areas. Help me to feel peace and joy from You. Thank You for the citizens of Fort Worth. Protect them, help our little town to grow and prosper into what You want it to be. Give us wisdom and courage."

She paused and spread her hand across her stomach. "If I am . . . if I do have a new life in me, I give it to You. Direct this child in Your ways, from his very beginning to his very end. I'm afraid to hope or think that I am for fear that I'm not. Make Your ways my way; I am Yours and You are mine."

Liz looked to the cemetery where her grandfather's body lay beneath the soggy dirt. She recalled a verse that she had returned to often after Caleb died. "But this one thing I do, forgetting those things which are behind, and reaching forth unto those things which are before, I press toward the mark for the prize of the high calling of God in Christ Jesus. Rejoice in the Lord always: and again I say, Rejoice."

Liz knew with certainty her grandfather really wasn't in the ground but in heaven. "One more thing if You would, Lord. Please find Lucas Mailly today and tell him I miss him and love him." Her eyes pooled with tears and she wiped them away. She took one last look down the road toward the ranch. Only the raindrops dancing in the ruts of the silent street were present.

Thunder clapped as Liz dressed, freshly braided her thick blonde hair, and prepared to face her day.

※　※　※

Emma was the first person up at the house that morning. Usually she was the last to grace the kitchen. She looked at the cold stove and silent teapot. She pulled her shawl across her shoulders and looked out the window by the kitchen table. She saw a lamp glowing above the mercantile and knew that Liz was up and about. She followed the glow down the back staircase and to the back room of the store. Liz opened the door and quickly pulled in a few small logs to dry and then her image disappeared from Emma's view.

Emma had come to know her cousins better over the past months and found that she greatly liked them—not just loved them because they were family or inspiring women but truly liked them. They were hardworking, ingenious, and unafraid of adventure. She wished that she had had more time with her grandfather as well. She could feel that this dauntless attitude came from his beliefs and teachings. Maybe if she had known him better and sat at his knee like they did, she would feel more comfortable with the person she was deep down. Liz and Megan let her be herself. They weren't always trying to mold her into their image like her mother and sister, Abby, did.

Megan and Emma enjoyed long uninterrupted talks as they worked in the kitchen together. Megan was always so fun-loving that she even made the hottest days of canning tolerable. They laughed over the simplest things time after time. Emma loved every moment with her cousin Megan.

She heard the door open and Liz was there smiling and shaking a few raindrops from her cloak. "I about froze to death last night! I didn't know it was going to turn chilly. I didn't have the stove ready or a quilt on the bed, and with Thomas gone, it was just plain cold." She looked at Emma with a wrinkle from her raised eyebrows. "Guess I'm going to have to get a dog to keep me warm at night."

Emma chuckled. "Good morning. Did you have any dry wood inside to scare out the cold in the store?"

"Yes, yes I did. I got the stove downstairs started and came right over for food. Now that I'm up, I'm definitely hungry."

Liz got the stove fired up and put the teapot on. Since Thomas was gone, the coffeepot stayed empty unless they were expecting a guest at their table. "Are the other two still asleep?" Liz asked as she started breakfast. Before Emma could answer, Liz said, "I think we need a Texas-sized breakfast this morning."

The skillet clanked on the stove as Liz started to heat it. Emma smiled. "You are hungry. Sorry I didn't have breakfast started. I just came in myself. The overcast sky sure can trick you into staying covered up in bed."

"Yes, I know," Liz exclaimed and reached for a bowl with several brown eggs in it. She was working quickly and didn't try to keep the noise down.

"Okay, okay, we are up!" Megan and Abby came into the kitchen pulling their wrappers around them tightly and hugging themselves to gain a little warmth.

"Good." Liz smiled over her shoulder and put a piece of buttered bread in her mouth. "I have something exciting to tell you."

Abby cleared her throat and looked at Liz. With her forehead wrinkled, she willed Liz the courage to tell the others about her baby.

Liz turned and looked at them all.

"I spoke with Katie Longmont yesterday and we are going to have a wolf hunt! Tonight!"

"A wolf hunt?" Liz was so excited she couldn't talk and cook at the same time, so Emma took over the duties and stirred the eggs in the skillet.

Liz explained about Samuel's friends coming from the city and what the men would be doing. "So." Liz pulled the list from her apron pocket and read what Katie had written. "Our part is to bring several sweet dishes that we are becoming so famous for around here, and our quilting. Anna has her two frames if we want them. She is going to be piecing on a new quilt top for the church. I saw her design when she was in the mercantile and it is lovely. She is not using scraps but actually bought a length of fabric in black and pink. She has named it Fort Worth Star."

With that news given, Liz popped another bite of buttered bread in her mouth. She chewed and watched as each woman considered her news. By now, they were sitting at the table with teacups in their hands, sipping and stirring in a little sugar.

"Well," Abby said, now wide awake, "I've never been to a party given in honor of a . . . wolf," she stammered.

Megan leaned over and whispered to Emma. "But I have been to a few parties with wolves!"

"Megan," Abby scolded out of habit and then smiled at her humor.

"We're going to have a full moon, too." Liz spoke quickly and tried to add a bit of eeriness in her voice.

Emma looked to the window. "What if it is still rainy?" she worried.

"It doesn't matter. Jeremiah said that they can track better in the soft mud," Liz replied and set the last plate of food before the women. "He does want the cloud cover to be scattered as they need the light of the moon."

"Where's Luke?" Emma asked. "Should we wake him for breakfast?"

"He took Leon over to the Parkers. Anna not only helped Mrs. Perkins nurse his father back to life but she needs to get ready for hosting the quilting tonight. I'm sure it's hard for Mr. DeJarnette to be still and heal; he'll be eager to go back to their ranch. Anna said they have excellent horse stock. Luke is interested in seeing their place one day."

Liz looked at the window where the rain made little trails on the glass and continued. "It's too bad they'll miss the fun today, but the main thing is if Mr. DeJarnette's head and leg wounds will heal cleanly. I'd never met their family before."

"I met them on one of my first family visits," Abby said. "They have a beautiful ranch and the horses are gorgeous, grazing on the hills. Mrs. DeJarnette, as you saw yesterday, is a lovely lady with fiery red hair and green eyes and creamy skin. I know she got quite a shock when Pastor Parker sent old man Jeb out to their place with word about the accident on the bridge."

"Old man Jeb, wasn't he the one who had the county records?" Megan asked. They all laughed and were amused at how this old man seemed to appear whenever there was excitement in the settlement.

"I think that I would like to start on a new quilt, and I'd like it to be a Christmas pattern. I have lots of red and green scraps. Liz, do you have some muslin?" Abby asked, her eyes shining at the plan.

"Yes, come get what you need. Will you be able to relax at the quilting? Are you all ready for Monday?" Liz asked.

"Yes, I am ready to ring the bell," Abby answered joyously.

"Well, guess we need to prepare for a fun weekend," Megan said. "None of us have ever been to a wolf hunt quilting before."

CHAPTER 11

The mercantile was slow during the morning and early afternoon. Liz used the time to prepare her sewing project for the evening. She sketched out her block using triangle-shaped units and flying geese. She pulled down a basket from the top shelf and sorted out some fall colors of gold and brown fabric scraps. She placed a half-used spool of thread in the basket with her favorite pair of freshly sharpened scissors. From her sewing display, she chose two new needles and packed it all in the basket. By midafternoon, the main road was busy and bustling with excitement and activity. The rain had let up and only a few puddles scattered about in a rut were evidence of the overnight and morning shower. The earth was warm and dry and seemed to drink in the moisture. The day stayed cool and only a few gray clouds lingered. The air bristled with excitement. Wagons were lined up and down the street. It seemed everyone had come to town for the weekend.

Mr. Wilton and his wife, Fanny, sat in the back of their wagon with their baby boy, Vernon. Fanny had a quilt spread out where the baby napped as they ate a late lunch. She smiled fondly at the sight of her busily exploring seven-month-old finally tiring out enough to sleep.

Mrs. Perkins, of course, was a part of the quilting fete even though she had no menfolk in the wolf hunt and sat outside the mercantile window on a bench. She visited with each family as they arrived. She set her quilt basket at her feet, her bonnet casually pushed to her back.

Tex, Jackson, and Colt rode into town and tied their horses up in front of Samuel's law office. Samuel was on the wooden walk with several men Liz had never seen before. She wasn't aware when his friends had arrived. She stayed at the window watching with anticipation as the crowd grew by the moment. Zeke Goodwin staked out an area close to Anna's house and started up his fiddle. He played song after song from memory. Smithy came walking from the livery all cleaned up and looking good. He had his harmonica in his hand. Zeke saw him coming and nodded at Smithy to start right in. Zeke's red hair bounced as his foot tapped out a tune. Smithy had no problem joining in.

Parker and Luke had arrived home safely from the DeJarnettes' and helped Anna and Little Dove prepare the meal. The tables were all set up under the canopy of trees behind their house. Colorful quilts, some tattered, were used as tablecloths as the food started covering the table. Lemonade and drinks were on one end with sweets and the like on the other. Meat, potatoes, and vegetables of all sorts filled another table, and the aroma of fresh bread drifted throughout.

Megan and Emma were now at Anna's adding additional utensils and plates to the table.

It seemed everyone was here except the Longmonts and Thomas. Liz didn't even know if Thomas knew about the wolf hunt or if he would be home. She wouldn't allow herself to be sad and lonely with so much fun to be had. She took her work apron off, smoothed her braid, and locked the back door. Liz went to the front and flipped the sign over to "Closed" and stood outside by Mrs. Perkins.

"Well, what are we waiting for? Let's go to the party!" Liz picked up her own basket of sewing supplies that she had prepared as well as Mrs. Perkins's basket and proceeded down the steps to cross the street.

"Aren't you going to lock the door?" Mrs. Perkins asked as she stood to follow.

"Oh." Liz gasped and ran back to turn the key in the lock. "My excitement for the festivities has made me absentminded." Liz and Mrs. Perkins gathered the baskets she had left on the side of the road.

"It is going to be a lot of fun," Mrs. Perkins exclaimed. "It has been a long time since I came to town for a quilting bee. The wolf hunts have been a social event around here for a couple of years now, ever since Mr. Smith showed up to be with his family."

Abby joined the other two women and the three continued to walk the path to Anna's and the churchyard. "How long has Mr. Smith been around here?" Abby asked.

"Must be three years. This is our third hunt, so we can say it's a yearly event. Everyone has so much fun. I think it is because we don't have to stop at bedtime. We go all night, and then cook breakfast when the men get back after the hunt. They relive the details of the night to the women and each other, boasting about the event. Sometimes a child will hear them arrive and come in all sleepy eyed. They'll sit all curled up in their mama's lap and imagine the wolf growling at the dogs."

"Oh," Abby said. "I see how we could all look forward to this every year. At least, the food and friends."

Mrs. Perkins smiled. "Don't worry about that ole wolf, Miss Wilkes. He gets away every time!"

"They don't catch the wolf?" Abby was confused. "If you hunt, don't you catch or kill what you're hunting?"

"That is what I asked Katie," Liz said. "And she didn't seem to care or know either."

"You two act like city girls, and I know better than that," Mrs. Perkins said with a wide smile.

The group stopped in the middle of the street. Zeke's hunting dogs were tied to his wagon and started to bark at the women. Abby took a step away from the dogs and one pulled his rope taut as he lunged at the group.

"Let's keep walking," Mrs. Perkins said. She steered Liz and Abby around the pack of dogs. Zeke whistled from where he played the fiddle and the dogs retreated to the wheels of the wagon. Liz looked over her shoulder to make sure the dogs were staying put. She moved her sewing basket to the other arm closest to the dogs.

"If there has been a problem at any of the ranches along the Trinity, then they may kill the wolf, but mostly it is just for fun for those rich city men. They pay pretty good for the excitement. Then they have a tall tale to take back with them." Mrs. Perkins was matter-of-fact with her comments.

"Who are they?" Liz asked.

"Not sure. Mr. Perkins was already gone when the hunt started, so I was never introduced to any of them. But I hear they are important men from Austin. Last year Sam Houston planned to attend!"

"Did he come?" Abby was now intrigued. Maybe she could meet someone who would be interested in adding funds to help her school.

"Nope," Mrs. Perkins answered. "But plenty of government bigwigs have been here before. Mr. Smith has some real important friends at the capital. Bankers and doctors too."

The group made it to Anna Parker's house where the party would take place. Abby and the others had been to Anna's gatherings before. She was a wonderful hostess and, feeling as excited as children at Christmas, they couldn't wait to get there.

The tables and food were in the back behind the house where the trees offered shade and shelter. Anna's two bedrooms were ready with extra quilts and bedding for any children or adults who couldn't make it through the night. Smithy and Zeke played music that made the children dance.

Abby looked down the street toward Samuel's law office and saw a large group of men scattered across the wooden walkway. Samuel stood with two other men she didn't recognize as they smoked fat cigars. In their fancy jackets, they reminded her of the Mississippi gentlemen from her hometown. She wasn't impressed. Jackson, Colt, and Tex stood with a few other men she didn't know and they all had glasses of amber liquid. She was sure it was expensive liquor. Her father had a smoking room in their plantation home where the men would gather and discuss issues of the day. Cigars and alcohol were in abundant supply at her father's. The sight on the sidewalk and her memories left an uneasy feeling in her stomach. It made her upset with Samuel and she wasn't sure why.

"Abby," Megan called at the door, "come help us with the quilt. We only have one to go into the frame. It's Fanny's and so lovely."

With all the food prepared and ready, the women could focus their attention on setting up the quilting bee. Fanny's quilt wasn't too big. It had cream background fabric, cut from a dress of her youth. She named it Broken China. When she came west, her mother had given her all her china dishes and packed them in her fabric scraps. When she arrived at Mr. Wilton's farm and unpacked her things, almost all of her mother's dishes were broken. She tried to glue them together, but to no avail. There were just too many sharp points on the broken and shattered pieces. But she did use the fabric scraps to piece the quilt.

Fanny, Megan, and Abby pulled the quilt across the frame snugly and pinned it into place.

"Fanny, Emma and I are going to quilt at the frame with you," Megan told her.

"That's wonderful. I hear that you two are fast. With an all-nighter, we may get it done." Fanny picked up her crawling baby and pulled a stick from his fingers. "This one is Vernon. He's seven months old. I swear he is so chubby because he puts everything in his mouth. Just this afternoon, I broke a canning jar and he made his way over to the broken glass before I could get it all cleaned up. He sat in the middle of the sticky peaches just as pretty as you please and didn't even notice the cut on his knee." The baby jabbered and pulled on his mother's ear. "He has been teething. I hope he isn't fussy tonight."

Little Dove came over and took Vernon from his mother. "Don't worry, Mrs. Wilton. Daisy and I have games planned for all the little ones. I'll take him over with the others."

Little Dove looked at Abby, who was now finished pinning the quilt. "Daisy thinks we can play school."

Abby smiled and laughed a little. "Well, don't get them so smart they don't show up come Monday."

Little Dove disappeared out the back door where Abby heard

squeals of delight from the children. Jeremiah and Katie Longmont were arriving in their wagon. Their three children scampered out the back of the wagon on their own. Daisy went to the backyard first, where she and Little Dove started arranging the play classroom immediately. Daniel and Lillie weren't too far behind her.

Katie placed basket after basket of food on the table. Anna helped and gave her a hug. "Thought you might have brought another wagon with so much food here!" Anna joked.

"Oh, Anna, I can never outdo your cooking. Your dishes are always so delicious."

Anna smiled and gave her another hug. "Now that you are here we can start. Did Jeremiah go to gather the menfolk?"

"Yes, they will be over to eat any moment now." Katie and Anna smiled at the children playing as they walked into the house where the other women were.

"Welcome, Katie! The fun's about to begin," Megan sang out. "What are you sewing tonight?"

"Well," Katie said. "I want a small Christmas table quilt. One that will run through the center of the table."

"Oh," Megan said, "what design will you put on it?"

"I have it sketched out here." Katie placed her sewing basket on the table and took a piece of paper out of the corner. "See, a winter scene of a schoolyard." Katie looked at Abby. "It is their first year at school. It will be a Christmas memory."

Abby looked at the drawing. "How clever you are using triangle pieces to create the picture. I would have used appliqué for all of those tiny pieces."

"Not me. Appliqué is not my friend," Katie exclaimed.

Several ladies laughed at Katie's remark and understood. Not many could put down appliqué like Abby.

"I have a Christmas quilt I'm going to start piecing myself tonight," Abby said.

"Well, we are all thinking about cooler weather, aren't we?" Katie said as she went to see the other sewing projects.

They heard the men arrive. All cigars and liquor had been left at Samuel's in respect of Anna Parker. She had stood her ground at the first wolf hunt that these would not be in her home, and no one objected. No one would dream of disappointing Anna Parker.

Pastor Parker stood next to his wife and led the group in a prayer. He blessed the food and asked God for a safe hunt and for the wolves to be speedy. His *amen* was met with a few chuckles.

Samuel thanked Anna for hosting the event and Katie Longmont for the organizing, preparing the food, and cooking all week. Samuel's guests from Austin voiced hearty "thank yous."

"Thank you, Mr. Smith," Katie stated. "Please lead your friends first through the food tables."

Conversation and laughter filled the room as Katie looked for her friend Liz.

"There you are. Sorry I haven't told you sooner. Jeremiah sent word to Thomas about the festivities. We waited as long as we could but we didn't have word back from our ranch hand. I'm sorry, Liz." Katie searched Liz's eyes for signs of reassurance. "There's no need to worry."

"Thank you, Katie. You did all you could do. The cattle and starting the ranch came up so quickly we didn't really have time to talk about or think about all the different things. He really didn't tell me how long he would be gone. In fact, I don't even know where the ranch is except that it is on the other side of your land."

"I'm sure he is a lonesome cowboy, Liz. He will be back soon." Liz smiled at Katie's reassurance and the two women joined the others at the food tables.

Dusk was approaching and with a full meal in their bellies, the men were prepared to go. Guns, bullets, and packs were lined up and ready. Zeke went to get his dogs while everyone gathered out front. Children squealed with excitement under the glowing moon rising in the east.

Dogs howled in anticipation of a scent. Zeke had them on ropes and took a wolf pelt out of a pack, shook it at the dogs, and let each one get a good smell. The dogs pulled at the ropes and barked, climbing over each other. Zeke unleashed them and commanded, "Hunt." Dogs scattered into the trees behind the church and schoolyard. The long legs of the men pulled them up the hill and into the tree line following the dogs. It all happened so quickly. A flurry of activity and then they were gone. Only a deep howl of a dog could be heard in the distance.

"Well," Megan said in the sudden silence, "let our quilting begin!"

The children ran back to their game of hide-and-go-seek in the schoolyard and the ladies washed the last few dishes. Emma covered the leftover food.

Liz sat down and started to cut out her brown and gold flying geese. Fanny asked about her quilt and Liz showed her the drawing. Fanny liked the idea of adding four appliquéd wreath blocks to the middle of the quilt top.

Katie and Abby sat close to Liz and started piecing their new ideas for Christmas projects.

Fanny sat at the frame and directed her helpers in the design of her Broken China quilt. Megan, Emma, and Mrs. Perkins listened carefully and then started to lightly draw the lines on the quilt with chalk.

Anna came into the room and plopped into the empty chair. "Do any of you mind if I just rest a few minutes before I starting quilting?"

"Of course you may," Katie replied. "Thank you again for your help. You are always so good to help out. Did you have time to plan a sewing project? You were so busy with Mr. DeJarnette and the wolf hunt back to back."

Anna smiled. "Yes, I did have a busy week." She reached for a basket of soft yellow yarn and pulled out a half-crocheted baby bootie. "I thought I would pick up where I left off last winter." Anna glowed as she looked at the room of women.

Mrs. Perkins was the first to react. "Anna, are you with child again?"

"Yes," she beamed, "and I am further along than I have ever been before. I'm thinking it could be an early Christmas present."

The room was a flurry of well wishes and hugs as they congratulated Anna on the news.

Katie grinned and said, "Well, I can't hold it in any longer, either. My next baby will be here the end of January!"

"Oh my," Liz exclaimed, "it must be in the water!" Liz looked shocked at the news of two pregnancies. She didn't say a word about her own possible condition.

Abby and Anna waited to see if she would say anything but she didn't. Liz was beginning to think she might actually be . . . well, maybe having a baby? But did Thomas even want children? He had often remarked how happy he was with their little family of each other and Luke. Liz felt a bit of disquiet at the thought that there might be another coming.

CHAPTER 12

Anna tiptoed into the room to check on the sleeping children. It was the wee hours of the morning and they were all fast asleep. Their sweet little faces poked out from under the quilt. She admired their perfectly shaped rosy lips and chubby cheeks. She whispered a prayer for each child and then one for her own.

"Lord, thank You for giving me another chance to have a child. Please bless this one with a long and healthy life."

Their dog, Angel, raised her head and blinked at Anna. She then stood and gave a soft, rumbly dog greeting.

"Are the hunters coming back for breakfast?" she asked as she gave the white dog a pat. Angel was a pet and would have been useless on the hunt. Anna rose and listened but she didn't hear anything.

"The children are all sleeping soundly," Anna told the parlor full of quilting women. Angel followed her out and went to the door. "I think Angel hears our hunters coming back," Anna said.

Mrs. Perkins glanced at the clock ticking on the wall. "It's a might early. I'm not ready to put my needle down and start breakfast. We have almost run out of room to stitch on Fanny's quilt. We can't quit now with it so close to being finished."

Emma looked over the quilt to see how much was left. She ran her hand over the open area left in the middle. Soon she would run into Megan's completed area.

Angel put her front paws up on the door and whimpered. "Maybe she just wants out," Megan suggested.

Anna opened the door to let the dog out and saw Luke's dog, Bear, running in circles with excitement across the porch. Angel barked and wagged her tail just as Thomas appeared from the dark. He held one finger up to his mouth for Anna to be quiet.

"Liz, come see what Bear has found," Anna said.

Liz stood, stretched her arms and shoulders, and walked reluctantly to the door. In her years of experience with animals, she knew that anything could be dug up for approval. She cautiously looked down at Bear and saw boots. Her eyes traveled up the legs and to the face of Thomas. He held open his arms and she flew into them.

"Hello, Liz," he said and kissed her.

"Thomas, I didn't know if you would come." Liz didn't turn loose of her hug.

"I came as soon as I could. Liz, I love it at the ranch. I can't wait for you to see it."

"Well, when will I?" she asked.

"Soon, I'll take you soon." He kissed her again. "I've missed you."

"I've missed you too. I about froze to death last night!" Liz teased. "I considered getting Bear to keep me warm."

Thomas chuckled and led Liz back into the house. "Good mornin', ladies, how's the quilting going?"

"Hello, Thomas," he heard in unison.

Bear and Angel settled down under the table where Thomas and Liz now sat with cups of fresh coffee. Liz was still determined to try to develop a taste for it.

Liz got a good look at her husband and exclaimed, "You look like you've had a black eye! What happened?"

Thomas told her about the incident, making light of it. He made it a humorous story so she wouldn't worry about him.

"Then tell me about the ranch." Liz took a sip and put the cup back down quickly. It was too hot.

"You won't believe how incredibly beautiful it is." Thomas looked at Liz but she could tell he was seeing the ranch. "Even with fall upon us, it is green. The trees are scattered about on rolling hills with plenty of creeks and streams tucked in. The water is plentiful and clear. We won't have to dig many wells to water the livestock. The herd looks so beautiful grazing out on the pasture land. The longhorns are really gentle, elegant creatures."

Liz brought him back with her interest. "Tell me what you've gotten accomplished." Her elbow was on the table and her chin propped in her hand. Her eyes were starting to get sleepy now that she had gotten still.

Thomas smiled as he looked at her. "Here, drink your coffee so you can stay awake with me." He pushed the cup closer to her. "It took almost two days to get the herd to our grazing land. The grass was so deep it was easy to keep them in the area. They just ate and ate. Buck seems to have the most knowledge about cattle. He said—"

"Which one is Buck?" Liz interrupted.

"The one Emma encountered and robbed." Thomas laughed.

"Oh." Liz nodded her head and smiled. It was good to have Thomas home. She reached for his hand.

Thomas wrapped his fingers around hers. "Buck and I decided to start branding first. We can let them graze around in the same spot since grass is plentiful. The rain spooked them a little but the cowboys started singing a lullaby and calmed the herd right down." Thomas shook his head remembering. "It was the strangest thing I ever saw. All these boys singing those huge animals with long horns right into relaxation."

"What song was it?" Liz asked.

"Something about little doggies. Guess I am gonna have to learn it." Thomas chuckled. "We really have only been out there a short while but much progress has been made on the corrals and barns. We moved the herd and started branding. All the guys are going to stay on until winter. Buck and Clyde are brothers and they for sure want to stay on indefinitely. Buck would be a great foreman if Chet doesn't want to stay."

Thomas took a drink. "When will Chet and the freight wagon be back? He doesn't even know we have a herd."

Liz quickly thought of her loyal friends and employees. Chet, Blue, and John had worked for her grandfather at the Louisiana timber mill. They had helped with their trip west in the wagons and now worked in her freight business. These men were as close as family to her and she trusted her life and family to them.

"Next week. Chet will certainly be surprised that you have a herd all rounded up. He thought that the two of you would be doing that together." Liz thought for a moment. "Will he want to stay on with the freight line for a while or go on out to the ranch with you?"

"Not sure, but he is a cowboy born and bred. We may have to find another hand for the freight line. I'll ask around and see if anyone is looking for work."

Liz certainly didn't want her freight line slowed down. She wasn't prepared to lose Chet just yet. She would do some asking around on her own. A frown wrinkled her forehead because everyone she knew already had work.

"Don't start worrying about it already." Thomas rubbed the wrinkle above her eyes.

"I'm not worrying," she answered. "I'm working out a solution to the problem." She smiled but noticed a slight annoyance in Thomas's eyes. She quickly added, "Or I'll leave it to you to figure out," and was rewarded with a special wink from her husband.

✕ ✕ ✕

Megan and Emma stood up to stretch when Mrs. Perkins said that it was time to roll Fanny's quilt. They would be able to finish it and even start the binding. Almost everyone would stay through Saturday. Pastor Parker planned a Saturday night message and a sunrise service the next morning as well. Then the wagons would start on home after all the leftovers were eaten. Monday would bring a new work week and the first day of school.

Anna had three blocks cut out and two completely sewn together. They were beautiful and were sure to brighten up the pew in the front row of the church. She decided to put a little bit of gold in each star and that sparked it right up.

Liz had six of her eight blocks cut out and one appliqué block pinned together. Around midnight, she had taken some time redesigning the quilt. It was always good to have several talented seamstresses working together to brainstorm an idea.

Katie and Abby had several Christmas fabrics of red and green put together, as well. It had been a highly productive gathering.

None of the Mailly women had ever had an all-night sewing event and were thrilled with the extended fun and friendship. Liz realized this was pretty much the only family Mrs. Perkins had. Everyone was content to catch up with the news in each other's lives. Emma's often bored face was actually glowing, so she was enjoying herself despite her private prediction to Liz earlier.

Emma went to the table where Liz and Thomas continued to talk. She coaxed the pot's last bit of coffee into her cup.

"Emma," Thomas said, "I have good news for you."

She stopped the cup halfway to her mouth as her eyes asked, "What?"

"Buck, the cowboy you fussed with about his horse? He found another horse he liked at the Longmonts' stable and told me to tell you that he would sell Gypsy to you if you still wanted her."

Emma would have jumped out of her pointed-toed black boots if she had them on. In fact, Thomas looked around the room and noticed that all the women were in their stocking feet.

"Gypsy." Emma said the word like she was considering it. "I like that name. He didn't tell me she had a name!"

"So . . . are you going to keep her?" Thomas asked.

"Yes! How much? Did he say?"

"No, but I'll make sure he gives you a fair price."

"Thank you, Thomas!" Emma gave Thomas a hug and a kiss on the cheek. She swirled around the room making her skirt fill up with air as she twirled on her stocking feet.

Abby watched her sister and thought she was the happiest she'd seen her in quite some time. She pushed away her inclination to tell her she wasn't behaving like a lady and just smiled instead.

Thomas decided to leave the women to finish their work. Angel and Bear followed him out the door but stayed on the porch sniffing the air, ears perked up at the night sounds. The evening had a comfortable temperature; only a slight jacket or long sleeves would be required. Thomas was glad that the rain was over. He had spent too many days and nights in wet clothing over the last few months. It was a feeling he didn't enjoy much, but tonight was perfect. A lone wisp of a cloud drifted across the full moon.

Suddenly a piercing cry from the house shattered the quiet and Thomas turned quickly.

Fanny Wilton had her baby boy on her shoulder and was patting his back. He was screaming in pain. Anna went to Fanny to see if she could help. She took the baby in her arms and cooed, trying to soothe him. But the little one arched his back, his legs pumping frantically.

Fanny took her baby back and rubbed his tummy. But Vernon continued to cry at the top of his lungs. His mother carefully laid him down to change him, checking each diaper pin to make sure none were open and poking the wee one. Once she saw they were all secure she folded down the diaper to take it off and gasped at what she saw. "An—Anna!" Fanny quavered. "Come quick."

Anna came running with a warm wet cloth to pacify the baby. She had it twisted to form a nipple and dipped it in sugar.

"What is it?" Anna asked. Then she saw the bloody diaper. "Fanny, what happened?"

"I don't know." Fanny tried to calm the baby who cried and kicked his legs desperately. Tears filled her eyes.

"Fanny, hold his legs still so we can see where the blood is coming from," Anna said, trying to be calm. Fanny held her baby so Anna could clean his bottom and find where he was hurt. As she cleaned, she found no harm on the little boy. The chubby baby continued to wail and wiggle desperately almost out of his skin. All of the women and Thomas were now gathered around the squirming infant inquiring about his condition.

Vernon's cries and the fussing women had awoken some of the sleeping children. Little Dove stood at the doorway with the sleepy-eyed children gathered about her. Not one foot was over the doorway threshold but all of the little ones were confused and looking about. Little Dove held a child who lay on her shoulder sucking his thumb. Her other arm rested on the shoulder of Daisy as she snuggled closer to her older friend. Silently they stood waiting for the wails of little Vernon to subside.

Liz asked, "You couldn't find any place that he was hurt?"

"No," Anna and Fanny replied at the same time.

Fanny bounced and patted her little Vernon.

Megan asked, "He was fine until now? He hasn't been fussy or feverish?"

"Yes, only a little teething," Fanny insisted. Her voice trembled.

"Has he ever had blood in his diaper before, with or without the teething?" Liz asked again trying to backtrack on the mystery of why this baby was hurting and bleeding.

"What did he eat earlier this evening?" Megan asked.

"Just what the other children ate," she replied.

Suddenly Katie spoke. "Fanny, did you say earlier that you broke a canning jar and Vernon crawled into the mess and started eating the peaches?"

"Oh, my! Yes," Fanny cried, "he must have gotten into the glass!" She took deep breaths, trying to contain her rising panic.

Anna took the baby from Fanny. He stared up at her, his little knees pulled up to his stomach while he still shuddered with sobs. Anna blinked back her own tears as she looked into his eyes, trying to give him relief and comfort from his pain. He began to calm down and took the sugar nipple Anna placed at his lips. He was quiet for a moment.

Liz spoke first. "If it is glass in his belly, we can only wait and try to comfort him the best we can. Fanny, can you calm yourself to nurse him?

If he has something in his tummy, it might soothe him and help him pass it."

She nodded and wiped at her tears. She couldn't speak.

"Good. Emma, do you still have some lavender poultice that you made for the horse?"

"Yes," she nodded.

"Good, go get it from the house to put it on his tummy."

"Anna." Liz saw that she was already putting on her boots.

Anna raised her head. "Yes, Liz, we will go to the church. Where two or three are gathered together in My name, there I am in the midst of them," she recited from Scripture.

Fanny held her baby close and looked at each woman. "I've never been this frightened."

Liz took Fanny by the shoulders. "We will pray for the peace which passeth all understanding. You hear?" Fanny nodded. "We'll be right next door at the church. Send for us if you need to. You have plenty of friends right here to be with you."

✳   ✳   ✳

Emma ran home to gather the poultice for the baby, who was still whimpering but becoming worn out. Emma applied the pack of medicine to his tummy. It was warm and the baby looked up at Emma when she applied it. Emma prayed silently and Fanny sang softly as she rocked. Tears rolled down to Fanny's lace collar. Emma had to turn away from what she saw before she totally broke down.

Liz gave one last order as she and Anna headed to the church for a prayer vigil. "Mrs. Perkins, do you mind helping Katie, Megan, and Abby get breakfast started? Our hunters will be back soon."

With that said Liz and Anna shut the door and hurried over to the church. Anna lit the new candles on the altar chest and the two prayer warriors went boldly to the throne of God for little Vernon Wilton.

Suddenly, the night's silence was no longer a comforting companion.

CHAPTER 13

At least two hours had passed since little Vernon's cries first sliced through the night. The candles on the altar chest burned low and wax puddled around their bottoms. Liz stood up from where she had been on her knees, face bowed down. She pulled some hair back in place and sat on the step beside the big chest. In the semidarkness, she looked for Anna.

Anna was sitting in the front row, still and silent, staring straight ahead in her own thoughts. Liz got up and went to sit by her side.

"Are you all right?" Liz asked. She saw the bewildered look on Anna's face.

"I don't understand why God allows our little ones to be harmed," her friend replied. "Why is it so hard to bear a healthy child and keep him safe until he is grown?" Liz suspected she was thinking not only about Vernon but her own babies who had not lived.

"I don't know. We just have to stand on the promises in the Bible and keep going forward," Liz said calmly as she put her arm around Anna's shoulder.

"What promises do you mean?" Anna used her hankie to dab at her nose.

"There are many, from Genesis to Revelation. Romans 8:28 says that all things work together for the good for those that love God. In another place God says, 'I will never leave thee nor forsake thee.' And my personal favorite during hard times is more of a battle cry. It is found in 2 Corinthians 4:8."

"Tell it to me." Anna was looking at Liz with admiration.

"Basically it says that we get knocked down time after time and we don't understand, but we get up again and keep going."

"Thank you, Liz." Anna looked seriously at her. "As the pastor's wife, I'm the one who usually comforts others. Sometimes it's good to be the one receiving comfort. How did you come to such a strong faith?"

"When I was a very little girl, I stood looking at the flames that consumed my home with my father and mother burning inside. I saw a white-robed man step out of the fire and come to me." Liz licked her lips and continued. "He spoke and I heard Him just like you are hearing me now. He said, 'I love you and will always be with you.' He held out His hands and I saw the scars on the palms of each one. Then He said, 'I will keep you in the palm of My hands and work it all for the good. Believe in Me.' Satan tries to steal from us when we face hard times. But God gives us promises to strengthen our faith and build us back up."

Anna blinked, listening intently as Liz continued on.

"I still hear that voice and I have no choice but to put all of my faith in Him. I always try to work everything out on my own, but in the end, it is all up to Him. We fight and scratch out the life we think we want or need. But it is really useless and a wasted effort. We are ships without a rudder if we truly do not have faith in God."

"Is that when you and Megan were sent to your grandfather?"

"Yes. All of our things were burned in the fire. Megan was just a toddler; they found us in our nightgowns with Granny's appliquéd poppy quilt wrapped around us. The pastor's wife made us each a green dress, and then they put us on the stagecoach to go to our grandfather's house in Louisiana, not even knowing if he was able to take us in . . . or even still alive."

Anna felt stronger and more encouraged. Liz had been through so much and had built up a strong faith. "So a promise from God proves His faithfulness and love."

"Yes." Liz smiled and patted her friend's hand. "And I'm not saying it's always easy to be strong in the faith. When Caleb died . . . and when Grandpa Lucas died I struggled mightily, believe me."

Anna looked thoughtful.

Liz said, "Let's go see about the others and check on little Vernon and Fanny."

Mrs. Perkins was stirring the eggs in the skillet when Liz and Anna walked in the door. "Troubles come in threes," she asserted. "First Lucas, then Mr. DeJarnette—it's a miracle that man didn't drown—and now little Vernon."

Thomas sat at the table with an empty breakfast plate. Mrs. Perkins, Abby, Megan, and Katie told Thomas about the accident at the bridge as he ate.

"And how's the baby?" Liz asked, looking for a pot of hot tea and pulling up a chair next to Thomas.

Katie smiled. "He is sleeping, not too restless, and the bleeding looks to have stopped."

"Good." She plopped in a chair at the table and looked at Katie. Liz reflected how much more difficult this night would have been for Fanny had she been isolated at their place rather than here with a close group of supportive women.

The clock ticked on the mantel. Abby was ready for this night to be over. At least they had each other to help and lean on. She wasn't sure if Fanny could have gone through this alone.

Abby thought about all of it. "Liz, this is a perfect example of what my mother always talked about and how important female friendships are in our lives."

Liz remembered clearly how her aunt, Katherine Wilkes, had expressed her opinions about the friendships of women. She had sat in the parlor with a glass of fresh lemonade and spoke with Abby and Emma about life and marriage. She had placed her glass on the china tray with a sober glance at her daughters.

"Don't forget your sisters, the other women in your life. They will be more important when you get older. No matter how much you love your husband and children, you still need women friends in your life. Spend time with them, do things together. Laugh and cry together. Women will be the mainstay of your life. Time will pass, troubles will come, children grow up, work changes, love grows stale, men disappoint us, hearts break, and parents die. But no matter what, there will be a 'sister' to reach out to. We will weep together and cheer each other on. Sometimes they even break a rule for us. Women are the stronghold of life and will help you soar, not limp through your life."

Abby and Emma had watched their mother as she took a drink from her glass. Both had listened intently to what their mother was saying. Katherine had continued, "Abby, Emma, you are going on a great adventure. It is your life, in Texas or wherever. You have no idea of the incredible joys or sorrows that lie ahead. You will need each other and other women."

Liz had never heard anything like it before. Her aunt sounded strong and wise. She had always thought of her as a diffident type, quiet and behind the scenes, supporting the men. This speech sounded like a true Mailly woman. Liz could see the teachings of her grandparents in Abby's mother as never before.

✕　✕　✕

Abby was just about to fall asleep when the first sounds of barking dogs came through the trees. It was 4:45 a.m. and the hunt was over. The men and their dogs were finally on their way home.

Thomas pushed his chair back from the table and went to the door. He winked at Liz as he opened it and went out. He could hear the howling of Zeke's dogs in the distance as they got closer. He was exhausted and wanted to close his eyes for a few minutes. He settled in a chair on the porch and leaned his head to the wall of Parker's house. It just took a moment and he was fast asleep.

"Thomas, when did you get back?" Samuel kicked the leg of the chair, startling his friend, and Thomas jumped. His hat fell to the porch as he got quickly to his feet.

Samuel laughed and patted the sleepy man on the back. "You missed the excitement," Samuel told him.

"I missed the hunt but not all of the excitement," Thomas objected. "Mrs. Wilton's baby has taken ill. The women were all in a flurry and the little boy was screaming at the top of his lungs. Good thing he wasn't mine. I wouldn't know what to do. I'd better find Wilton and let him know what's going on."

Samuel looked around. It was all quiet at the moment. He couldn't see Mrs. Wilton or the baby through the window, only several women busy in the kitchen. The wind blew through the porch and Samuel tucked one hand in his pocket.

The men and dogs broke through the clearing. Zeke had both dogs tethered. They pulled at the restraints and went up on their back legs in protest. Zeke took them to the back side of the wagon and calmed them down slightly.

"They don't want to be done with the hunt," Thomas said as he watched.

"It doesn't help any when we have a wolf pup among us," Samuel said, as Luke came through the trees carrying a baby wolf in his arms. The little ball of fur was terrified, his yellow eyes peeking out from under Luke's arm. The pup was shaking and digging into Luke's jacket to hide.

"What in the world?" Thomas asked, now fully awake.

"They said I could keep him! Raise him and take care of him. I promise, Thomas. I will do it all."

"Who said you could keep him?" and his voice was stern.

Luke stood before Thomas on the steps of Pastor Parker's house. The hunting party was gathered behind him.

Samuel spoke first. "The mother was found dead in a trap." Samuel motioned over to where Zeke and Smithy put the limp furry body of a wolf in the back of the wagon. The long bushy tail dangled over the side, its bristles slowly fluttering in the wind.

"This pup is about starved; one other was already dead. We aren't sure if this one will even make it." Parker had walked up and took the squirming wolf pup from Luke and held it out for Thomas to look over.

"This won't work. We need to let nature take its course." Thomas shook his head. "We can't go into the wild and bring back a wolf to raise. They just don't mix well with civilization. I'm sorry, Luke. We can't keep it."

"But why?"

"I'm sorry, Luke," Thomas said again. "I've made my decision."

"Why should I have to do what you say? You're not my real father," the boy muttered.

Thomas was surprised. He had thought Luke was adjusting well to the marriage and to having a pa again.

The men's eyes went back and forth between Thomas and Luke. They knew this was a family matter and didn't interfere.

Liz stepped out of the doorway to stand by Thomas. She took the shaking fur ball in her hands. She cradled it in the crook of her arm and tried to calm the creature, tugging on the scruff of its neck to avoid being nipped. She stroked the soft fur and the pup began to settle. Liz felt conflicted between seeing how much raising this pup meant to her son and her loyalty to her husband. She chose her words carefully. "Luke, it's hard to interact with wild animals. He is a baby now but will grow into what he was created to be—a large, meat-eating pack animal. Thomas is just trying to make it easier on you."

Luke wasn't happy with what he heard. He stood up straight and eyed his parents. "I know that, but we aren't even sure if he will live. We might not have to worry about him growing up. We just can't leave him to die," Luke pleaded.

"I'm at the ranch. I don't have time to work with a wild animal," Thomas pointed out.

The sullen look on Luke's face was not customary for him.

Thomas shook his head again. "Luke, look at me."

Luke did so reluctantly.

"Son, you're asking for trouble. You are going to get hurt over this sooner or later."

Samuel made a suggestion and placed his arm on Luke's shoulder. "How about the two of us work on this together? The pup can stay with me. You can come over to help out. I will oversee the two of you. Thomas, what do you think?"

Liz looked at Thomas to see what he was thinking. Thomas just shook his head again. "Won't work, but if Samuel is willing to help out—" Thomas shifted his weight to the other leg and kicked at a dirt clod. "I guess you can try."

He had his arm around the waist of Liz, as Samuel took the pup under one arm.

Samuel scratched the pup on the head and pulled him up into one arm. "Looks like we're gonna be pals, buddy. Luke, see if you can rustle up some food for this little fur ball."

Luke hustled up the step past his parents and into the kitchen. The smell of breakfast waltzed through the open door and circled around the hungry men.

Jeremiah slapped Samuel on the shoulder as he walked by. "You're a good man, Samuel."

Out of Luke's hearing, Samuel replied, "I hope I did the right thing. It meant a lot to the boy, but he also needs to respect Thomas as his new father."

Samuel and Luke found a box to put the pup in. As Luke put food in for the baby wolf, he gave it a little pat. "JoJo. I'm gonna call you JoJo."

The tables began to fill up with the wolf hunters and heaping plates of tempting biscuits and bacon.

Thomas and Liz lingered on the porch after the rest of the group went inside. Liz leaned her head against his shoulder. She could hear his heartbeat. It felt good to be close to him. He pulled her closer and gave the top of her head a kiss.

"What next?" she asked.

Thomas pulled away and put his hand under her chin and raised her face so he could see her eyes. "Whatever is next, we will get through it."

"What do you think about the baby, Vernon Wilton? What if he swallowed glass?" Liz's voice betrayed her concern and the effects of the long night.

"I'm not sure what'll happen. He seems to be settled down now."

Thomas could see Pastor Parker and Mr. Wilton as they walked over to the house where Fanny and the baby rested. "But if he really has a piece of glass in his gut, it can't be good. I once had a dog that got glass in its belly, and—well, no use talking about that now. Wow, even a little guy like Vernon is a big responsibility."

Liz didn't need to respond since Emma was walking among the tables with a pot of fresh brewed coffee. She poured the steaming liquid in each cup and listened closely as they recapped the wolf hunt for the women. She found an empty chair and thought she would just sit for a minute. She wasn't sure when she dozed off but felt the warmth of a quilt placed across her shoulders.

Megan sat by Jackson with Samuel and Abby across from them. Katie and Jeremiah were seated next to Samuel's friends. The three visiting men sat in a row at the end of the table. Their chairs were casually pulled out where they could cross a boot over their knee. They leaned in when the story got exciting. One man would talk, and when he paused, one of the others would continue the wolf tale. Tex, Jackson, and Colt were at the other end of the table where Emma now dozed.

"Think she will fall off?" Jackson asked.

Colt looked Emma's way and smiled. "Hope she does, might be funny."

Jackson smiled but his eyes shot his disapproval to Colt.

"Augh, I'm just teasing. I won't let her fall."

Colt pulled up the edge of the quilt that had slid down one shoulder. He thought she looked very young as she slept. Her lips were slightly parted and her eyelashes fluttered. Colt thought that she might wake up and catch him staring at her, so he directed his attention back to his friends retelling the story.

Mrs. Perkins came out of the kitchen with the last plate of hot food. She had heard the tales before and was just happy to be needed.

Bacon, scrambled eggs, and biscuits disappeared as the plate was passed down the table. Colt eagerly snatched up the last biscuit. Jackson shot another scold at the younger Ranger. When Colt wasn't looking, Tex snagged the biscuit. The old man didn't even crack a smile as he downed it. Colt looked down and saw the empty spot on his plate where he was about to pour the honey. Jackson laughed as he watched Colt search for the culprit, his eyes checking out each plate. Colt never saw his boss brush crumbs from his shirt.

The mantel clock chimed 6:30 and the orange tint of the dawn was beginning to announce a new day. Abby heard the faithful rooster. Normally, everyone would be thinking about the responsibilities of the day before them. But not today. It wasn't long before the group found comfortable locations in and around the Parkers' house for a Saturday morning snooze.

CHAPTER 14

Abby was the first to wake up Monday morning. Her side of the bed was perfectly placed for the early light to stream down on her as it broke through the leaves and branches of a Texas red oak tree. It was a pleasantly warm morning. She sat up in bed and stretched. It was the day she had been waiting for, the first day of school. She rubbed her eyes and looked around. The house was dark and still. The sleeping Emma rolled away from Abby's side of the bed and pulled the quilt back up. Abby had unknowingly moved the cover when she sat up.

Abby quietly slipped out of the room and went into the kitchen to start breakfast. Well, at least the hot water for tea. She looked out the window toward town and all was quiet. The rooster gave a good long crow as Megan came into the kitchen fully dressed.

"Good morning, schoolteacher!" Megan sang. "Did you finally get rested after our exciting weekend?"

"Yes, I feel good." Abby smiled back. "Do you mind if I go get dressed in your room? I didn't want to wake Emma. It was such a long weekend. I thought she needed to rest a little longer after she worked so hard in the kitchen."

"Yes, go ahead," Megan answered. "There is fresh water in the pitcher."

Abby gathered her things together quietly and tiptoed out of her shared room. She heard Luke waking up as she closed the door to her cousin's room.

Abby took extra care to pin her hair up firmly. She brushed her teeth an extra time, washed her face, and pinched her cheeks for a little extra color. She smoothed out her navy blue dress with its crocheted collar made by her mother. She looked into Megan's mirror and smiled at her reflection.

Liz and Thomas had already come down from their room above the mercantile. They were having their morning drinks on the porch, but after a few sips of coffee, Liz poured the rest of hers into a flowerpot. "I just can't like coffee no matter how hard I try. I am going in for some tea. Would you like me to bring you out some more coffee?" She wrinkled her nose at the word.

Thomas smiled and nodded. "Thank you."

Liz returned with her tea and Thomas's coffee. She was feeling fine this morning. Not even tired after the hectic weekend of activity. If she had been expecting, she wouldn't feel so good this morning. Her suspicions had to be wrong, as she rather hoped. What if Thomas's encounter with the rattlesnake had turned out differently? What if he had never come back to her? It had been hard enough to care for Luke after Caleb had died. She wouldn't want another child to be without a father. Still . . . babies were a blessing, she mused.

"Thomas, did you know Anna is expecting a baby, close to Christmas?"

"No." Thomas drank and rocked slowly, careful not to slosh the hot liquid. "Hasn't she lost several?"

"Yes, but she is excited. She said she is further along this time than any of the others, so she thinks she will do well this time."

"Good," Thomas said as he swayed back and forth. "They are good people, and they're already great parents to Little Dove."

"Do you see Katie Longmont much when you are out at the ranch?" Liz sipped her still too hot tea.

"Not really. They have a big spread, as is ours."

"So you are unaware that they are expecting as well?" Liz asked.

"Sounds like a baby boom is coming to Fort Worth." Thomas put his cup to his lips.

"Yes, she is due mid-winter."

"I am sure Jeremiah is excited as well. He is a great father. The little ones don't scare him any."

"What do you mean?" Liz looked at Thomas.

"Oh you know. Those tiny ones, like Vernon, the other night all upset and crying like he was. I wouldn't have a clue what to do."

"Not a clue?" Liz repeated. "You underestimate yourself. Thomas, did you ever think about having children of our own?"

Thomas looked at Liz as though she were green. "No, with things like they were . . . are, never thought on it." Thomas paused. "I like it the way it is. I know what to do with Luke. He can ride and talk." Thomas laughed. "They need to all come about his age, even if he's a little moody these days. Anyway, you told me that after Luke, the doctor said it was unlikely you'd ever—"

Emma came out the door, breaking the conversation. "Thomas, do you know where I can get some chicks and a henhouse? I need to build a henhouse and get a rooster or two."

Thomas chuckled. "You're starting a . . ."

Emma finished for him. "Yes, I am starting a business. I need some chickens, a henhouse, and two roosters. I'm going to sell the eggs and provide chicks to people who need them," she repeated, "and sell fryers. Even thought I might open a food establishment. Might as well get paid for all the cooking I do around here."

"I see," Thomas said, thinking on her plan. "Guess we do need a restaurant here. You will do fine. Would you like for me to gather some men and plans to help? I will be leaving soon, going back to the ranch."

"I have the plans. I just need some manpower for a few days."

"Okay, I'll talk to a few. What will you pay?"

Emma thought on it for a moment. She didn't want to use her money. "I will pay by giving them free meals, according to the work they do."

"Sounds fair; I'll send some your way."

"Thank you." Emma tied her apron on and went back to the kitchen.

Liz was listening to Emma and Thomas but was still thinking about Thomas's comments on babies. She guessed it was a good thing she wasn't in a family way. Probably. Anyway, it was all over nothing. Anna and Abby certainly had her thinking along that line. Liz laughed to herself.

Thomas looked at Liz. "What are you thinking about? What's so funny?"

"Oh, nothing. Anna and Abby were just teasing me about having a baby, too."

"What?" Thomas stopped rocking and turned to look at her.

"Don't look so frightened, Thomas." Liz smiled. "You know Luke is all we have."

※　※　※

Abby hadn't been in her classroom long when Tex appeared in the doorway.

"Good morning, teacher," he said with a chuckle.

Abby looked at the weathered and wrinkled Ranger. He wasn't a big man, but he had the confidence of Jackson. His gun was at his hip, as usual, since the seasoned lawman was always ready for trouble. Tex had taken a protective role over the Mailly women after the death of their grandfather. He had lost the chance to care for his own daughters years ago.

It seemed a lifetime ago. He had been so foolish to act on his wanderlust and walk out on his family with no explanation. When he finally got the sense to return home to see his wife and daughters, it was far too late. It never occurred to him that they would give him up for dead and make a good life without him. They had not only survived but flourished.

Tex would never forget the day he rode up to his ranch. How many years had it been, anyway? He saw grown women who appeared to be his daughters and a new man standing by his wife watching grandchildren play with a litter of puppies. Laughter drifted over to him as he remained undetected in the grove. Finally he had ridden away from all that he had once loved and worked for, never to return.

Seeing after the Mailly women helped him atone for his past mistakes.

"Just tell me when, and I'll ring the bell," Tex said, turning away from his haunting memories.

"Thank you." Abby walked closer to him.

"Your grandfather was a real special man. You girls and the school were very important to him. Learnin' for these young'uns was a high priority. He was right proud of you and all the schoolin' you earned."

He paused and looked at his boots. He clicked his lip a few times before he started talking again. "I would like to have the honor of ringin' that school bell. I know he would have been here to do it and see each young'un enter your doorway of learnin'."

Abby sensed the lawman's wistfulness. She suspected he had secrets but would never ask. "Mr. Tex, thank you for that nice speech. It would be an honor for me." Abby reached out and patted his arm. His grin lit up his kind face, shadowed by the ever-present cowboy hat.

Her small group of students began to gather in the schoolyard. Peter Graham was first to arrive, wearing some of Luke's hand-me-downs. His hair was greased and slicked over to the side. Abby noted that he did not carry a lunch pail.

Luke was walking over from across the street. He waved as he saw Little Dove at the porch of the Parkers' house. She came down the walk and met up with him, her skirt jingling with the Indian jewelry sewn to it. They both had lunch pails in their hands.

Luke and Little Dove would be her only students of much age. Nat Turner, Thayer Tate, and Leon DeJarnette wouldn't be at school for several more weeks, not until harvest was over.

Katie Longmont drove her wagon into town and dropped off her three children, Daisy, Lillie, and Daniel. They had decided to let Daniel have a try at school. Due to his age, attending school was trial and error at this point.

Georgia Odessa and Leanna Wheeler were the last two little girls to arrive. Georgia's dog, Vera June, came to school with her, as it went everywhere with her. The dog always found a spot in the sun near the water pump and waited for her owner.

Abby smiled and nodded to Tex giving the approval to ring the school bell. The children crowded around by the steps when Tex pulled on the rope and the bell rang out announcing that school was in session.

"Daisy, how is your mother?" Abby asked as they lined up.

"She is good. She said the baby is kicking so much he wears her out."

Little Maxwell Cooper was a farm boy with big ears. He had been waiting on the school steps as Daisy spoke with the new schoolteacher. Maxwell always said what was on his mind and the first day of school was no different.

"My mama had a baby. It was her last baby. She told Papa no more babies. If he didn't take her to see the doctor in the city, he could be sleeping in the henhouse." Maxwell shook his finger in a comical imitation of his mother.

Abby raised her head to see what was happening. Maxwell Cooper was telling the whole schoolyard personal information. She had to stop him before he went on.

"Maxwell," Abby called out a little too loudly. She steadied her voice. "Please line up, and no talking as we enter the school."

Little Dove kept her head down. Luke looked around to see just what he had missed. Tex pulled the brim of his hat over his face and moved away from the students so they wouldn't see him laughing.

Abby didn't need any more color in her cheeks, as she could tell from the warmth that she was flushed. She was rather glad that the older boys weren't in class today.

Little Maxwell marched proudly into the school, set his lunch pail on the shelf, and found a desk to sit at. He was unaware that he had unnerved his teacher so early in the day.

Leanna Wheeler sat next to Maxwell Cooper. "How many babies does your mama have?"

"I'm the oldest of seven kids and I'm eight years old," Maxwell said with one thumb cocked in his suspenders.

"Class! Students!" Abby hushed the class. "It's our first day, so let's go over a few classroom rules."

After the morning hours of reading, writing, and arithmetic, it was lunchtime. Abby gave her lunch to Peter Graham. She made a deal with him. She would bring a lunch for him and in return he would keep the blackboards clean, wood chopped for the stove, and the floor swept twice a week. "We all need to work for what we have." She remembered Grandpa Lucas had said that to her more than once, and anyway, she doubted Mr. Graham would allow Peter to accept charity.

Abby was about to call the students back inside for the afternoon session when a shrill scream echoed from the schoolyard. The hem of her navy skirt caught under the edge of her chair as she stood up quickly. She heard it tear as she moved away and hurried to the doorway. There she saw Maxwell Cooper chasing the three little girls. How he kept up with several running and screaming girls, she wasn't sure.

"Maxwell! Stop that!" she scolded as she went down the steps.

Maxwell turned around at the sound of his name. There on the end of a stick was a wiggly dried-up snakeskin. It danced on the stick and swayed toward Abby.

"Oh, my!" She gasped and drew back. Her hand flew up to her crocheted collar. "Luke, please come here and take that slithery thing away where we won't be able to find it again!"

Luke was laughing. "Yes, ma'am." He took the stick from Maxwell Cooper and headed to the trees behind the church and school.

"Ladies!" Abby tried to calm the girls who were hiding out behind her torn skirt. "Come here." Abby was trying to bring the girls around to the front of her. She leaned over and looked directly into their faces. "If you don't react to the boys' teasing, it won't be any fun and they will quit sooner or later."

Instantly Abby knew that she should take her own advice. She made it too much fun for Samuel and the others.

She looked up and saw Daisy Longmont crying over by the new

storm cellar. "What has gone wrong now?" Abby whispered to herself. A frontier school certainly brought different challenges than her old position in Mississippi. She turned to go find out and that's when she saw blood running down Daisy's arm.

"Oh my!" she said loudly. "Maxwell Cooper, go get help right now. See if Miss Anna is home and tell her we need bandages."

Anna and Samuel heard the racket from the schoolyard and were already halfway there when they saw Maxwell Cooper running and yelling. Samuel grabbed him by the back of the collar to stop him. He held him up, his little feet still moving but going nowhere.

"Miss Abby said bring bandages and come quick!"

"Who is it?" Anna asked as they moved to the schoolyard.

"Daisy Longmont, lots and lots of blood!" Maxwell panted as he gave the news. The boy was filled with importance at his errand.

Anna and Samuel doctored up Daisy's arm. It wasn't as bad as it looked. It was easy to stop the bleeding and they only needed to put two stitches close to her elbow. The brother and sister were an experienced doctoring team. Daisy was an easy patient; she bit down hard on the stick that Abby placed between the student's teeth.

"It's going to burn some," Anna said as she poured the clear moonshine on the girl's arm. It trickled down her elbow and dripped off just as tears fell from her pink cheeks. Her eyes were wide and scared but she didn't move a muscle. "You are going to feel a tug," Samuel said. "You might want to close your eyes." Daisy blinked twice, then closed her eyes as she was told. She hardly felt Samuel pull the needle and thread through two times.

Abby wrote two new rules on the blackboard.

1. No playing on the storm shelter.
2. No playing or teasing with snakeskins.

✳   ✳   ✳

The close-knit community continued to pray for the Wilton baby and hoped for word that he would be fine. Anna and Liz both thought about their conversation the night of the wolf hunt. It was difficult to understand the bad things that happened, but they knew these things are part of life on earth—in heaven there is no pain or illness. Or death. They could and would remain faithful to the Lord whatever happened.

Mrs. Perkins had spoken to Mr. Wilton on the night of the wolf hunt, preparing him for the worst. She had said that if the baby had indeed ingested glass, it was possible that damage to his internal organs would occur, which would most likely be too extensive to recover from. She had advised him to keep the baby as comfortable as possible, cuddling and tending to him, praying and singing over him. She also reminded him to tend to Fanny.

Pastor Parker brought Anna out to the Wiltons' place midweek to stay with Fanny. When he came back he told Liz soberly that the baby had grown feverish and went between pitiful wailing and longer and longer stretches of sleep.

At the end of that week, Pastor Parker delivered sad news about little Vernon Wilton to the townsfolk.

After several days, he died quietly in his mother's arms. Anna was on hand to lay out the baby, and a small group gathered late in the afternoon to sing and pray at the gravesite. All hearts were breaking as they looked at the tiny pine box. Fanny leaned into her husband's shoulder, pale as a ghost. She looked as if her own soul had reached its end.

Anna reminded the other women not to try to comfort with a plati-tude such as, "you can have more babies." Anna knew other babies would not replace any she had lost. There was nothing more painful than bury-ing a child, no matter how many others might be in the family. Anna prayed, commending her friend to God, praying as she and Liz had that night a week before for the "peace which passeth all understanding." She intended to spend a lot of time with Fanny in the days to come.

She knew how it felt to lose your life and dreams and have to go on breathing.

CHAPTER 15

Several weeks of school passed without incident.

Little Dove and Luke were Abby's oldest students and would be until Nate, Thayer, and Leon were able to come. At least, Abby hoped Leon could attend school. Mr. DeJarnette was still not fully recovered from his leg and head wounds and was limited in what he could do at the ranch.

Luke and Little Dove got along well and progressed nicely in their schoolwork. Luke enjoyed his math and science and helped his friend when she couldn't work it out. Little Dove, in turn, helped him with literature and English, subjects Luke wasn't much interested in.

Luke also kept up with his chores at home, at the mercantile, and raising the wolf pup, JoJo. He was quite proud the pup had survived. Little Dove had been captivated by the wolf pup as well and gave Samuel and Luke a lot of advice on how to care for the wild animal. JoJo was also fond of Little Dove. The Indian girl had formed a bond with the animal that the others did not fully understand, the pup hopping and wiggling with excitement every time she came around. Little Dove would lie down and let him crawl all over her. She used a fur pouch she wore on her belt as a toy and played with the pup. Even Bear wrestled playfully with JoJo.

One day, Abby let the class have a short break outside. They were told to use the outhouse and get some sunshine. She would call them back in shortly. When they got back inside, it wasn't long before Daniel came up to Abby's desk to ask a question.

"I need to use the outhouse," Daniel said as he pranced by the side of her desk.

"Daniel, we just came in a little while ago. Are you sure you need to go?"

"Yes," he replied as he wriggled.

"Did you go when you were told or were you playing around and forgot?"

"Yes, ma'am, I went."

Abby looked at the little face. "Well, you must have a little bladder."

Daniel stood still for a moment and answered. "Yes, ma'am, it is only this big." He used his finger to show how long it was.

Abby laughed as she realized what he had said. Later, when she told Katie, they had a good laugh about his honesty, but decided he may not be quite ready to stay all day at school.

Daisy Longmont's stitches were out of her arm and she was doing fine. Daisy and Lillie were good natured, sweet little girls. Daisy liked to tag around after Little Dove and Luke, and they didn't mind. Lillie wasn't as far as they were in her studies, but was younger and knew that she would be at their level when it was time.

Lillie showed up at school one day with her bouncing curls all cut off. She barely had more than a shine of blonde hair on her head.

Abby had to ask. "Lillie, what happened to all of your beautiful curls?"

"Mama told us to go play so Daniel and I went outside. I was playing with my doll's yarn hair. Daniel said he would roll mine up like Mama's. So he sat behind me and rolled it on cockleburs. He wound it so tight Mama couldn't get my hair loose. She had to get her good sewing scissors and cut them out. It didn't hurt, I didn't cry," she told her teacher proudly, "but Mama just cried and cried as she cut. Papa wanted to spank Daniel, but Mama wouldn't let him." Lillie was as serious as she could be. She ran her hands over her head. "Mama said she would knit me a new cap come winter so my ears won't freeze off."

Thinking how Katie's next child was due in a few months, Abby said,

"Mothers certainly have their hands full. I don't know how she does all that is expected of her."

Lillie mixed in well and played with Georgia Odessa and Leanna Wheeler. Maxwell was their age but he didn't fit in well with either the three little girls or the older group. Abby did feel sorry that he didn't have boy pals his age and understood when he got into a little trouble.

Vera June, Georgia Odessa's dog, continued to come to school each day with the two little girls. It mostly waited at the water well in the sun or shade of the pump. Today was no different, but Abby could see that the dog was going to have puppies. She hoped Maxwell wouldn't notice and start talking all over again.

Anna's belly continued to grow and she was glowing with excitement. She felt healthy and positive about this baby.

Little Dove was excited to have a baby coming in the house. Sewing little gowns and booties kept them busy in the evenings. Little Dove had taken quite well to the crochet hook.

Liz and Thomas found a routine, too. He went out to the ranch each week and returned home for the weekend, confident he could leave the ranch with Buck and Clyde and several others who were continuing as ranch hands. Chet decided to stay with the freight line for the time being. Thomas was doing fine without him and Liz didn't want to lose Chet as a wagon driver. Liz finally dismissed the idea that she was carrying a baby. She wasn't tired or sick anymore, and her other symptoms had cleared up. She told Anna and Abby that they were wrong.

Life was good. They had plenty to eat and no other needs.

Liz had almost forgotten about her grandfather's gold from the sale of the family timber mill back in Louisiana safely hidden under her staircase at the mercantile. Lucas had wanted a ranch, and the money was for them to use in their new adventure. The mercantile was doing well, so Liz used her profits to invest in more inventory. She was glad that only a few others knew about the gold.

Thomas had gotten some money from an uncle and used it to buy his land north of town. He had also saved all of his money from working at the mill for so many years, and he used some of it to pay for his herd of longhorns and payroll for his cowhands.

The people of the settlement shared a lot of responsibilities and worked together well. Rumors and news of disquiet in parts of the country reached them, but the little town of Fort Worth, Texas, settled into a routine even as it was growing. It looked more like a town instead of a military fort.

A wagon train passed through quite often. The travelers bought supplies from Liz's store and restocked for their continued trip west. Many of the passengers had dreams of finding gold in California and along the West Coast. Liz listened to their hopes and dreams. One evening while she was working on her quilt, she pondered the desire for gold and decided to name her pattern Gold Rush.

Megan was content to run the house and do her sewing. Fort Worth just wasn't ready for a full-time dress shop, though she felt confident that the day would come and she would be busy as a bee. In the meantime, she fitted ladies and girls for dresses and even tried her hand at men's shirts for new settlers who didn't have womenfolk to sew for them.

Jackson was officially stationed at the fort and set up housekeeping in the old military bunk cabin. Megan and Jackson enjoyed their growing friendship and ate many meals together. They talked about Texas, books they had both read, and events from the news, and sometimes just enjoyed the silence as they sat on the porch. Jackson had never had a comfortable, companionable friend like Megan before; well, besides his horse, Zeus, and Megan was sure a lot prettier.

Emma bought the horse from Buck, who made a deal with her. In exchange for food and bathing rights when he came to town on the weekends, Emma didn't have to pay cash for her. She liked the name Gypsy, so she kept it. She felt that she had a gypsy spirit herself, wandering to and fro. She knew from the beginning that the two of them were meant to be together.

Emma had her henhouse built and bought several dozen chicks from local ranches. She worked out a schedule so that she would have eggs to use in her cooking and eggs to sell. Plus, she needed some of the chickens to grow so that she would have fryers to use and sell. She calculated the number of eggs per day for her use plus chickens to fry in her restaurant. Thomas had promised to bring two roosters home from the Longmonts' brood the next weekend.

Emma chose a building near Liz's store for her restaurant. It was close to her supplies, her home, and her henhouse. She swept, mopped, and thoroughly scrubbed the place from top to bottom in preparation for opening.

Thomas sent a couple of hands in to help her build a few things. Liz ordered her a new stove, dishes, and other supplies she needed. It was basic and simple, but Emma would make improvements as she went. She did have one section set up "tea-party style" for when the ladies were present.

Megan offered to sew the curtains for the café on her treadle sewing machine, so Emma chose a red print with white daisies inside a square. They were gathered at the top and pulled to each side of the long windows. With the sunshine streaming in and the cheery curtains at the front window, the place looked cheerful and welcoming. Megan agreed to help out, and Luke was available on Saturdays. Emma also said she could use Little Dove's help on Saturdays.

Liz and Abby observed that Emma was happy and busy these days, and expected that running the diner would prove to be a satisfying outlet for her restlessness.

Ranger Colt kept his post at Birdville but he wandered into Fort Worth occasionally. Emma talked with Colt about her new horse, Gypsy. She found out that his horse was named Bullet. Emma thought that Colt was joking. The names were just too similar with Colt being a make of gun and now his horse a bullet.

Luke was especially pleased these days. Not only was he thriving in school, his wolf pup had lived, though he still felt some resentment toward Thomas over that incident. But one day he had a surprise. Thomas and his mother presented him with his grandpa's horse. Millie was a special girl and he had been caring for her ever since Lucas rode into town months ago.

Nate and Thayer were now coming to school and rode in on their own horses each day. Now Luke would have Millie.

And one day Leon came riding in.

The older boys welcomed him with friendly slaps on the back, and Abby said, "Leon! I'm so happy to see you. Does your being here mean your father . . ."

"He ain't—isn't—completely healed up yet, Miss Wilkes," the lad said. "But he's getting better every day and he said it was high time for me to skedaddle to town for learning." Leon's grin spread across his face. "He's able to do most of the chores now."

Tex rang the bell for school each morning he was in Fort Worth. One day after school he wandered in and asked Abby if she would teach him to read. He never had the chance to learn and was eager to improve even at his age. So before she erased the board each afternoon, he would come by and get his lesson. It was easy to study while riding his horse. He said he didn't have much left to think about or occupy his brain anymore. Abby sensed he was lonely.

A week or two after his lessons started, Abby saw that someone was with Tex as he approached the school. To her surprise, it was Mr. Graham, Peter's father. He looked different than he had the last time she had seen him. Today his hair was neatly greased and combed, he had shaved, and his patched clothes were somewhat clean.

"Mr. Graham, how nice to see you again." Abby was unsure as to the purpose of his visit. She hoped he wasn't going to pull Peter from the school, not when he was settling in with the other children and flourishing in his studies.

"Ma'am." Mr. Graham glanced at Tex.

"Miss Wilkes," Tex began, "I wonder if you'd mind takin' on a second grown-up pupil. I was tellin' Graham here how I'm finally gettin' some learnin' and asked him if he'd join me. I hope you don't mind."

"Oh, that's splendid!" Abby smiled delightedly at the men. "I'm pleased as punch to have another willing student. Of course you may take lessons with Tex."

⁂ ⁂ ⁂

The news of the growth of Fort Worth was starting to spread and families continued to wander in, looking for land to buy and a place to call home. Samuel was as busy as he wanted to be with land deeds and homestead rights. He even acted as the judge on some occasions.

Abby saw her classroom grow as students trickled in. It seemed like families were moving in all the time.

CHAPTER 16

Each day continued to be more beautiful than the day before. Autumn brought warm days and cool nights. Abby thought the weather in Texas was perfect.

Election Day came on November 4 that year, and the town would be busy all day. The booths had been set up in the mercantile and the voting paperwork was all complete. An election board had been decided on, and Samuel, Smithy, Tex, and Parker were chosen to serve.

Emma expressed her annoyance that women didn't have the right to vote. She told her sister and cousins she felt the traditional female role wasn't much different than that of her papa's slaves. Her friend Nellie of course didn't have a say-so in the voting despite the fact that much of the election talk had been over the black slavery issues. Grandpa had been right about the growing unrest in the country. The other Mailly women actually agreed with her, but today it didn't matter because everyone would be busy, especially Emma at her restaurant.

She decided to name her place Emma's Table, and had spent weeks preparing for a busy election day. Sweets lined one table from beginning to end. There were pies, cobblers, cakes, and cookies of every kind. She had three different lunch dishes prepared as well as soups, bread, and potatoes. Someone told her it looked as good as a feast at the White House! She unlocked her door to a breakfast crowd that flowed down the wooden steps. Many had ridden all night to be present on voting day.

Megan took her pencil from her hair and said to Emma, "Well, let them in, let's get going."

Emma smiled at Megan and ushered the hungry settlers of Tarrant County into her establishment. They, along with the other women they had hired to work, were busy all day with people coming from far and wide to vote.

Abby started her school lesson that day on the history of voting and what it meant to the nation. She talked about the House, the Senate, and the president's responsibilities. Abby lectured on the candidates running for the presidency. The Republicans were a new conservative group whose candidate was John Frémont, an explorer who was nicknamed "The Pathfinder." Millard Fillmore was the candidate for the American Party, whom some called the "Know Nothings." The Democrat who wanted the office most was Stephen Douglas. But many felt he had made too many mistakes and blamed him for the "Bleeding Kansas" issues. James Buchanan was then pushed to the forefront of the Democrat party.

She thought she did a wonderful job presenting the lesson on a complicated issue. The older students were attentive and the younger ones at least grasped the basics. After her lecture, she let the students out for mid-morning recess.

"Stay close to the school. Remember, town is busy today." Abby issued the reminder as she gave the dismissal. Only a few minutes had passed by when Georgia Odessa and Leanna Wheeler came to the doorway.

"Miss Wilkes," Leanna called, "we can't find Vera June, and Georgia is crying."

Abby stood and went to the doorway where the two little girls stood. Georgia had big tears rolling down her plump, rosy cheeks.

"Georgia, did your dog come with you today?"

Maxwell was now on the steps surveying the situation.

"Teacher," Maxwell piped up, "you know that dog comes every day with Georgia. She waits over by the pump." He gestured to the water pump in the schoolyard. "See, no dog." Maxwell shook his head.

Georgia started to kick up the tears when Maxwell confirmed the point.

"Georgia, don't cry." Abby patted her student's shoulder. "Let me go and look around."

Abby stood and walked down the steps and into the yard. She circled around looking for Vera June and calling her. Maxwell stood on the steps with the two little girls. He put one arm on the shoulder of tearful Georgia.

"Your dog's gone. Vera June done run off, Georgia."

Georgia thrust her shoulder and knocked his arm off. She didn't want to believe what Maxwell said. She used her sleeve to wipe at her eyes.

Abby came back to where the other children were gathered at the steps.

"Have any of you seen Vera June today?" she asked.

"Just this morning," Nate answered. "Bet she got scared with all the extra goings on in town and went home."

This made sense to her, so Abby ushered the children inside to finish the morning lessons. "Georgia, don't worry, she will be waiting for you at your house when you get home today."

The spelling words Abby wrote on the board were all voting or government words. The older children were given more difficult terms written at the bottom of the board.

Just as Abby was about to lay her chalk down, she heard the first howls. Every few minutes, it would come again. The students would look up during the howl, and then go back to their spelling when it subsided. This went on for close to an hour and then little Maxwell Cooper started talking.

"I know what that is. Georgia Odessa's dog, Vera June, is having her puppies under the schoolhouse."

All Abby could think was, Oh please, no.

"My papa had a painted horse that had a baby. It came with two spots on its nose. It was an Indian pony. Papa couldn't get close enough to it to see if it was a boy or girl."

"Maxwell, finish your spelling!" Abby commanded sharply. "Keep working."

All the students went back to work. All was quiet for several minutes and Abby started to relax again.

Mrs. Perkins had finished the quilt she called Tin Roof. She had made it for the students and the school to keep in the storm shelter. Today was the day she was coming to town, so she packed it up and headed to the school. She parked her buggy and proceeded to the classroom. Just as she entered, the howling kicked in again.

"Bless my soul!" she exclaimed as she looked around the classroom.

Maxwell turned in his chair to pipe up with the news. "Georgia Odessa's dog, Vera June, is having her pups under the schoolhouse. Horses have two bottles. Cows have four. Don't know how many Vera June has."

Nate and Thayer burst out laughing at Maxwell. Luke and Leon muffled their amusement.

"Maxwell Cooper!" Abby exclaimed. "That is enough. Go sit on a church bench until I come get you."

Maxwell scuffled into the other room of the schoolhouse and sat in the front bench.

"Excuse me, class, while I meet with Mrs. Perkins." Abby walked to the back of the classroom where Mrs. Perkins stood with the quilt in her arms.

"I'm sorry, Mrs. Perkins. We are having an unusual day with the town so full and Vera June having her puppies under the classroom."

"Well, I guess so. Seems like Maxwell Cooper has spent a lot of time on the farm with his father and the farm life."

"Yes, it would seem. I know he doesn't mean to be so blunt. He just talks a lot. It is so matter-of-fact to him."

"As it should be." Mrs. Perkins dismissed the matter and handed Abby the mossy green quilt.

"Keep this at the school and use it as needed," Mrs. Perkins said. "Sorry it took me so long to get it to you." She smiled and was gone.

Maxwell stayed in the church, but not in the front row. It wasn't long before he was up poking around the table at the front. He found a drawer at the top, almost hidden from view, so he tugged it open. Seeing a bunch of papers, he took them out and laid them along the altar steps.

Vera June continued to howl every few minutes. The classroom was mildly quiet as Abby looked about. Her little class was working well despite the unusual racket. Abby walked around the desks perusing their work.

She made her way to the open area that went into the church. Maxwell had been so quiet she thought he might have fallen asleep. "Could I be so lucky?" she wondered. Before her she saw Maxwell settled on the altar step in the middle of some official looking documents.

"Maxwell," she said as she walked down the aisle toward him, "what do you have?" Abby stooped to pick up one. What she had in her hands were the Tarrant County records stolen from Birdville.

"Maxwell! Where did you find these?"

He looked innocently at his teacher. "Here in this drawer. What are they? Hey, are these the papers the men were fighting about? My pa was talking about it. They don't look that special to me."

Maxwell had his rabbit ears up again and knew just what was going on everywhere in the community. Abby briefly wondered what this young man would be when he grew up. Maybe a newspaper writer. He certainly did have a knack for nosing things out.

"Maxwell." Abby seriously and calmly called for his attention. "These are important and a big secret. No one is to know about them. It is so important that you tell no one. *No one.* Do you understand me?" She held his chin in her hand, compelling him to obey her.

"Yes, ma'am, I understand." He paused for a moment. "Could someone die if I told?"

Abby hesitated. "Yes, Maxwell, someone could even die. You must keep quiet."

"Yes, ma'am," Maxwell repeated solemnly.

Abby turned him loose and started to pick up the papers. She didn't know if she could expect him to do as she said or even understand the reasons for it.

"Go back to the classroom and continue your assignment quietly, please."

Maxwell went somberly to the others while Abby stacked the papers and replaced them in the hidden drawer at the front of the church. This was what the townsmen were up to before school started on that pre-dawn morning. The documents were to be kept in a safe, public place. The church was that place. The church, where people came in every week, where children had school every day. Now what must she do about it?

✕   ✕   ✕

Abby looked at the clock and wondered if the day would ever end. It was close enough to lunchtime that she decided to go ahead and dismiss the class for their dinner. She wasn't sure if the morning had been as productive as she had planned. The hustle and hum of town was a distraction as were the laboring howls of Vera June. Then Mrs. Perkins came by and Maxwell found the hiding spot of the county records. Just what, if anything, should she do about that? She walked to the window and looked out at her students eating their lunch.

Maxwell, Georgia, and Leanna sat on the steps with their lunch pails. Each time they started to take a bite of their food, Vera June would whine or howl again. Georgia was getting worried about her dog and started to cry.

Maxwell patted her on the back. "When I finish my lunch, Georgia, I will crawl under the steps and see if I can find your dog. She should be about done having those pups by now." He took a bite as he looked across to where the older boys were eating.

Georgia's eyes lit up. "Did you hear, Leanna? Maxwell will look under the school for Vera June."

Leanna asked, "What you gonna name the puppies?"

Georgia munched on a red apple, juice running down to her elbow. She was quiet for a moment as she licked the palm of her hand. "Penny Ann and Veronica Jane."

"What if she has a boy puppy or more than two?" Leanna asked again. Georgia shrugged her shoulders and looked in Maxwell's lunch pail to see how much longer it would be before he finished his lunch. She was extremely anxious for him to check on her dog.

Vera June kicked up the howling again. Leanna and Georgia looked at each other and then to Maxwell.

"She ought to be about done with having those pups. I went with Papa when the cows were calving last spring. They bawled half the morning, and then the calf comes out headfirst. Calves don't stand as fast as the baby horses do. Horses are up and ready to eat even before the afterbirth comes out. Sometimes a mare will even be standing and drop that baby right to the ground. Did you know that?"

Once again, Maxwell just spoke the facts of life right out to the little girls.

Georgia shook her head and looked at Leanna. She wasn't sure what Maxwell was talking about, but she was ready for him to go under the school and see about her dog.

Abby came to the door to call the students back in for the afternoon session. She hoped she could encourage them to complete a little more before the day was over.

Maxwell whispered to Georgia as they picked up their pails. "I'll go under after school. Vera June will be all done for sure." He nodded his head in confirmation.

The afternoon went more smoothly and quickly. Abby had almost forgotten about the dog fiasco. Only occasionally could they hear any racket coming from the bustling downtown. Before she knew it, it was time to dismiss her students for the day.

The older boys were out the door first. Nate, Thayer, Leon, and Luke ran up the street to Emma's Table. She promised them some work and they were excited to be in the middle of the action for the afternoon. Sitting indoors all day wasn't what the young men wanted to be doing on beautiful fall days. They came bursting in the door looking for their employer and the list of tasks. Emma and Megan were glad to see them as well. The dishes had piled up in the back and all of the tables in the front needed to be cleaned off as well as the floor swept. Megan was making more coffee and Emma was trying to control her curly hair. Her pins hadn't held well.

"How was school?" Megan asked as the young men tied on long white aprons and rolled up their sleeves.

"It was great! Georgia Odessa's dog had her puppies under the school today," Luke answered as he reached for the cookies and handed some to each friend.

"Yeah," Thayer agreed, "she howled all morning. It put Miss Wilkes on edge all day."

"Oh, well, I bet that was an interesting day." Emma finished with the last pin in her hair then clapped her hands. "Here is what I need you to do." She handed a broom and a list from her pocket to each eager young man.

"Did you hear?" Emma asked Megan. "Abby had some puppies born under the school today. I can't wait to get her side of the story. Abby's so prudish it must have been uncomfortable, to say the least." She laughed.

Back at the schoolhouse, Maxwell scooted on his stomach under the building. The sun's angle was just right for him to see well. He dug his elbows and knees in as he pushed forward toward the whimpering. Georgia and Leanna were on their hands and knees watching the best they could.

"Watch out for any old snake!" Leanna called out the reminder.

Maxwell stopped to look around and then moved forward some more. "I see them!" Maxwell called back. "She's got two."

Abby went around the school where she heard the voices. "Georgia, Leanna, what are you doing?"

The little girls stood and turned to face the teacher. They silently looked at her. Georgia had her arms straight at her side and Leanna twisted her pinafore with both hands.

"What are you doing?" she asked again.

They looked at each other and remained silent.

"Georgia!" Maxwell repeated. "She has two."

"Maxwell, where is Maxwell?" Abby asked and walked closer.

Georgia and Leanna stepped aside and pointed under the schoolhouse.

"Maxwell is under the schoolhouse? What is he—?" Then it hit her. Maxwell and the girls were looking for Vera June and her puppies. Abby bent down on her knees and leaned over to look under the schoolhouse. It was now all shaded and she couldn't see very far. "Maxwell Cooper! Come out from there right now."

"Yes, ma'am," a voice called back.

Maxwell scooted out backwards. The first thing Abby saw was his boots, legs, and then his backside. Abby was tempted to give it a good swat. He stood up between the two little girls. He had dust all over him and cobwebs coming off his ears, those big ears. Abby looked at each child before her and smiled. She started laughing, covered her mouth, and started laughing some more. Looking at the students, she shook her head and laughed again.

Maxwell, Leanna, and Georgia just looked at each other and then back to their laughing schoolteacher. Leanna still twisted her pinafore and looked like she would cry.

"Maxwell," Abby said calmly but firmly, "did you find Vera June?"

He nodded his head with big eyes.

"Does she have puppies?"

Again he nodded.

"Do they appear to be well?"

"Yes, ma'am, but I didn't get too close. She snarled at me and Leanna said to look for snakes."

Abby smiled again. What else could she do?

"Will it be all right to get someone to help get the puppies out so you can take the puppies home with you?" Abby looked at Georgia.

Georgia nodded her head. "We didn't mean to do any wrong."

"It's all right. You're just concerned about your dog. Go on home and I will bring her and her pups to you as soon as I can. She might have to stay there awhile."

Georgia Odessa frowned at the last bit of news.

"It will be fine. Go on for now and please don't get under the school anymore. There could be snakes. Leanna was right."

Leanna quit twisting her pinafore and the three ran off with their book primers and lunch pails. Georgia stopped and threw her arms around a startled Maxwell in gratitude.

What a day it had been. Now what would she do about those puppies? Abby wanted her quiet classroom returned. She decided to walk up the street to the mercantile and Emma's Table. She was in her own thoughts when she looked up and saw Anna, Parker, and Samuel talking in front of his law office.

"Better watch where you are going. Town's too busy today to be daydreaming as you go along," Samuel teased.

"Oh, I am well aware of the day's activities." Abby sighed and stopped on the boardwalk with her friends. The three looked at her weary face as she looked at each one of them.

"Are you aware that Georgia Odessa's dog got lost and then was found when she started to give birth under the schoolhouse?"

"What?" Samuel asked.

"Yes, we have puppies that need to be removed and soon, before Maxwell Cooper decides to give any more details on the birds and the bees."

"I see." Samuel chuckled. "Your students got more than the three Rs today?"

"Yes. How can we safely get the dog and her babies out? Vera June is a prize possession to Georgia Odessa." Abby was tired from the stress of the day. Now it all appeared funny. Her friends wanted more details of the day's activities and they all laughed as Abby relaxed and recounted her day.

Abby didn't mention anything about what Maxwell found in the church. She decided that she would speak with Pastor Parker about it later.

"Miss Wilkes," Samuel said, "I would be happy to help you with Vera June."

Abby was a little more relaxed with Samuel these days and she felt comfortable. She didn't give him any reason to tease her unnecessarily. She took her own advice that she gave the two little girls and it worked, most of the time.

"Thank you, Samuel. We need something to put her in so we can take her to Georgia's home. She doesn't live far and the dog is small."

Samuel went inside and got a small wooden box. He gave JoJo a pat as he went in the door. The little wolf yipped and followed him. "Hey JoJo, you have to stay. Luke is working this afternoon. He'll be over later to play with you." JoJo jumped up to reach Samuel but could only reach his thigh. He yelped as Samuel shut the office door.

"JoJo is growing," Anna said as she looked at the size of his paws on the glass windowpane.

Samuel looked at the animal yipping to get his attention. "He is training well, but can a wolf live on Main Street?"

"We all have our dilemmas, Samuel, and mine is first on your list." Samuel grinned at Abby and followed her to the school.

Abby looked back to see Anna again. She had her hand on the small of her back. Her belly was bulging under her skirt. Anna was getting closer to her delivery time.

"Do you know when Anna is due?" Abby asked as they walked.

"I would guess anytime in the next few weeks would be all right. She is concerned. Who wouldn't be, but she feels good and looks good too." Samuel was looking forward to being an uncle. In his book, little ones were meant to be enjoyed.

"Is Liz feeling well?" Samuel asked.

"Yes, why?" Abby didn't understand.

"Well," Samuel stuttered. They were now at the school and he put the box down. "Thomas was worried about her a few weeks ago and he mentioned that you and Anna thought that she might be . . . you know, with a baby of her own."

"Oh, Thomas told you that?"

"Yes, he was really worried about it. He said babies scared him to death. 'Would rather tangle with a rattlesnake' were his words."

"Well, looks like he has nothing to be concerned about. I don't think Liz will be able to have any more children. That's why he was so surprised at the possibility."

"Yeah, that's what Thomas said."

Samuel decided it was best to pull a few boards from the classroom floor to get the dog and her puppies. Abby watched as Vera June was pulled through the hole in the classroom floor and placed in the box. The dog stood and looked over the side as one puppy came up next. Samuel cradled it in the palm of one hand. He placed it in the box and Vera June lay down with her baby. Then he went back into the hole for the other puppy.

"This one is dead," Samuel said. "See? It's not breathing and is already cold."

Abby inspected the little dog in his hand. She looked down at Vera June licking her new baby.

"Do we tell Georgia or just let her think she only had one?" Samuel asked.

"She knows. Maxwell crawled under and saw two." Abby thought for a moment. "She needs to learn that death is a part of life. I will tell her."

Abby went to her desk and got a small pencil box, laid a hanky in it and Samuel tucked the little dead pup inside.

"I'll go with you to the Odessas' house," Samuel said.

Georgia was jumping up and down when Samuel placed the box on the porch with Vera June and her puppy. Abby told her about the dead one and gave the little box to her.

Georgia looked at the dead puppy and stroked it with one little finger. "This one was Veronica Jane." Then she rubbed the one nestled close to its mother looking for one of those bottles Maxwell kept talking about. "Penny Ann, this one is Penny Ann. It *is* a girl, isn't it?"

Samuel answered, "Yes, both girl puppies. I'll take care of Veronica Jane for you, and we'll let Penny Ann snuggle with her mother."

CHAPTER 17

The older boys in Abby's classroom were naturally full of vinegar and always looking for some excitement. After school, they had been running ahead of the younger girls as they walked home and nearly each day they played a different trick on their classmates. Today was no different. Even Leon, whose family responsibilities had matured him a little more than the other boys, hooted with the fun of boyish horseplay.

On each side of the dirt trail for a short ways was a fenced-off pasture. When the trail T-boned with another, it was then open range. Thickets of trees and brush were scattered along the road where it was easy for the boys to hide and scare the little girls as they passed by.

The boys were always amazed at how easy it was to put the fright in them. They would scream like banshees and run like their life depended on it. A slight breeze ruffled the wooded area making a short whistling sound.

Georgia Odessa turned to her friend, laughing about the kittens that played next to the school. "The yellow one scratched me," she said and showed the long red mark on the inside of her arm to her walking partner.

"I don't think the boys came along today," Leanna said looking around.

"Me either. Do you want to cross the pasture? I don't see Mrs. Perkins's bull either."

Both girls scanned the area and no one or nothing was about.

"I guess it would be okay today." Georgia Odessa blinked at the gust of wind blowing her golden curls all around.

Both girls walked to the fence, then dropped their lunch pails and grammar books over the side of one rail.

Leanna Wheeler climbed over and looked both directions again. "Maxwell stayed in town today waiting for his mother," she said.

Georgia climbed through behind her friend. "Yep, I saw him walk to the mercantile."

They heard rustling and Leanna jumped. "Don't worry, Leanna," Georgia said, gathering her leather strap of primers. "It's just the wind over in those trees."

The girls walked awhile not saying much, lost in their own thoughts, looking around as they crossed the corner of the pasture. Just as they got in the middle of their path the trees and brush began to rustle and bull sounds came from them. More movement and snorting started right behind them and the two girls took off running and screaming at the top of their lungs. They didn't stop to look behind them, certain that the pounding and snorting meant Mrs. Perkins's bull was hot on their trail.

Leanna reached the fence first and let the weight of her books pull her through the rails as she tossed them over. She turned to help Georgia and what she saw made her stop yelling and then turn red with anger. Georgia rolled over after hitting the ground and was trying to catch her breath when she saw that horns were coming through the fence.

There before her were the big boys from school with deer antlers in their hands. They were laughing and rolling in the grass.

"We sure scared the daylights out of you babies," they said, panting and laughing harder.

Leanna lunged through the fence and grabbed Leon around the neck with her legs sprawled around his midsection. The dirt dusted up as she repeatedly swung at him. "I hate you, Leon, you good-for-nothing rodent!"

Georgia poked her head through the fence. "Get him, Leanna!"

Nate easily pulled her off and said, "Calm down, Leanna. It is just a joke."

"Put me down, Nate! Put me down, you ole snake!" She got in a good punch on Nate's arm while Leon looked like a chicken had tried to scratch his eyes out.

Georgia calmly backed up to the fence and nudged her friend by the back of her torn jacket. They popped to the other side just as the boys turned to see Mrs. Perkins's bull coming at full force toward them.

"Yow!" screamed Leon as he scrambled to safety. Thayer did a high dive into the closest tree, leaving Nate to fend for himself.

He was still on the ground scratching at the dirt with his hands and feet trying to get a motion going in any direction. He was in luck as the bull headed toward Thayer, who was trying to go higher in the mesquite tree. The bull circled and snorted, kicking up dust with each threat.

The two little girls along with Leon and Nate looked like birds on a fence watching.

"Served him right," Leanna jeered. "I hope he never gets out of that tree." Her face was tear-streaked and dirty and her hair all a mess. "Come on, Georgia. Let's go home."

As the girls walked, they looked back to see all three boys not too far behind. Leanna was still mad as a wet cat. She stopped to watch the boys.

"What are they doing now?" Georgia asked.

Nate struck a match and threw it down in the dry grass, letting it burn some and then the boys stomped it out. They did this several times. Thayer struck one and let the crimson line of fire snake its way to each side and move forward as the breeze pushed it. It grew pretty quickly with the flames getting ankle high.

"Stomp it, boys, stomp it!" Thayer called to his buddies. "Don't let it get away." The breeze pushed it a little more. Then it hit a dirt row and the boys got it back under control.

Now the girls were close, watching it weave its way to the fence post.

"You boys are going to get in trouble," Georgia singsonged.

"Ya," Leanna added, "and I am going to tell on you since you scared the waddin' out of me."

"No, you're not, cuz we will haunt you every day after school."

"You already do, so there." Leanna stuck out her tongue and put her thumbs in her ears doing her share of taunting at the boys.

"You can see all over the grass where you boys have done this," she said pointing at the charred grass. "You're gonna get caught." Georgia repeated her future-telling thoughts. "You're not supposed to play with those matches. Your papa is gonna wallop the daylights out of you when he finds out."

"Well, he won't, cuz you're gonna keep your mouth shut," Thayer said back.

The next day after school Tex was waiting on the porch steps for the school dismissal. Abby welcomed him in and went to her desk for his new reading and spelling assignment.

Tex eyed the boys as they went past him, each one a little nervous as they hopped the steps and scampered around the schoolhouse.

"Do you think the old Ranger knows?" Leon had big eyes and was worried. His pa would put his thumb on him good.

"We didn't mean no harm," Thayer said confidently.

"I'm not so sure." Nate looked to see if anyone was coming around the corner.

They stepped closer to eavesdrop on the Ranger and teacher.

"Thanks, Miss Abby, thank you for teaching an old man to read," Tex was saying. "Me and Graham sure are beholden to you."

"You're welcome." Abby smiled at her oldest student.

"I also meant to ask you if any of your students have said anything about some fires outside of town."

"No," Abby said with a quizzical look on her face. "Why, what's happening?"

"I've noticed lines of burned-out patches. Saw a burnt match in one of them. Thought maybe your kids would have said somethin'."

"No, do you think some of my students are starting them? This could be serious; where exactly?"

"Close to the Perkinses' place."

"Oh, Leanna and Georgia walk that way. They would never do such a thing. Just a minute."

Abby walked to the doorway and looked for the two girls. She saw them talking to Nate and Thayer. Thayer had his finger poked in Leanna's face. When he saw the teacher he turned to run down the road. The two boys caught up with Leon who was ahead of them.

"Girls, will you come here a moment?" Abby asked.

Both little girls looked at each other and then the teacher. Abby was now very suspicious.

"It will just take a minute. Come up here."

Reluctantly, they went up the steps and into the coatroom at the entrance of the school.

Abby gave Tex a look as to show that she wasn't sure what was happening.

Abby's students now stood before her and Tex.

"Ladies," Abby started. "Is everything all right with the boys?"

Silently they nodded, looking from one adult to the other.

"Well, if you ever need to tell me something, you know that you can."

Both girls nodded again.

Tex scooted one boot on the wooden floor. "I've been noticing some small fires, burned rows on the Perkinses' road. Would you know anything about that?"

Each girl looked at the other and then back to Abby and Tex.

"No, sir," Leanna lied.

Georgia stalled and twisted her foot. "No sir."

Tex glanced at Abby and they both knew the girls had more information than they were giving.

"You walk each day down that road, don't you?" Tex bent down to their level.

"Yes," they both said.

"Have you seen the fires?"

"Maybe," Georgia said and Leanna gave her a scolding look.

"Well, if you do, let me or your teacher know. Someone could get hurt, the fire could get out of control, burn up a farm, kill some livestock." Tex stood back up and tipped his hat at Abby. "Thank you, ma'am," and was out the door.

Abby tried one more time. "Are you sure, girls?" she prodded.

"Yes ma'am," they said and went running to the Perkinses' road.

The boys were waiting for them at the turn just behind the trees.

"Are you girls tattlers?" Thayer barked at them.

"No," Leanna said and stuck out her tongue. Both girls raced home scared of the boys, the teacher, the Ranger, and the fire.

⁂ ⁂ ⁂

The clouds had started gathering the afternoon before and a cold rain started in the night. It wasn't winter yet, only the first morning in December and a few ice etchings were in the corners of the windowpanes of the mercantile. The frost was like dainty pieces of French lace. Liz was enchanted with the sight, and traced each pattern with her finger as she studied it. Somehow she hadn't thought that the Texas frontier could produce such delicate beauty. She thought about how pretty the pattern was and wondered if she could copy it for a quilting project.

She noticed a movement and peered out at the wet street. Pastor Parker was hurrying toward Samuel's door without a coat on. He only stayed a moment and then ran across the street to the mercantile. Liz opened the door for him.

"It's cold and rainy, Pastor, and you're all wet. What are you doing out?" Liz asked as she shut the door behind him.

"No time. Anna's water broke. She's been having pains all night. She wants you to come." Pastor Parker didn't look fretful, but kept his hand on the handle of the door; he wasn't planning on staying long. "Samuel's going for Mrs. Perkins. Little Dove wanted to stay, but I sent her to school."

"Of course; I'll get Megan to run the store. I'll be right over."

Liz quickly turned the lock on the front door and went to get her cloak. She hurried to the house and gave the news to Megan. Emma was already at the restaurant ready to serve breakfast to a small group of men passing through town. Liz noted earlier three horses that were tethered out front of Emma's Table. Megan was ready to go to the mercantile immediately. Her chores were complete and she had just sat down to sew red and green triangles on Abby's Christmas quilt.

She was looking forward to a cozy day of quilting. "It might be a slow day today with the weather. I would suggest that you take the quilt with you." Liz was gone before Megan could answer. She picked her way through the puddles in the street and pulled her cloak tightly around her.

Liz lightly tapped at Anna's front door and entered. The parlor was empty, but every lamp was lit. Thunder cracked and Liz jumped. "Get a hold of yourself. Think of Anna and the baby," Liz said to herself as she hung her cloak on a peg by the door.

Parker came out and said, "Liz, she wants you with her." Parker showed her into the bedroom, then went to the kitchen table, head bowed into his hands.

Anna was sweating even though it was chilly inside. Her hair was damp and she was at the end of a contraction. When it passed, she held a hand out for Liz. Liz went to Anna's side and held her hand. "How are you doing?"

"Good. I'm almost there." Anna squeezed her hand as another labor pain started.

Soon they heard the sound of the front door and Mrs. Perkins's unruffled greeting. "Take my wrap, there you are," she told Samuel. She took another look at Parker. "For goodness' sakes, you two get a cup of coffee. We'll take care of Anna."

※　※　※

The bell on the door of the mercantile rang and Mrs. Wilton stepped inside, shaking the rain from her bonnet. She had a basket in her hand.

Megan greeted her. "Hello, Fanny, it is so good to see you." She wrapped her arms around her, unmindful of the rain on her coat.

"Hello, Megan. It is good to be out even on this gray day. Actually, you're just the one I wanted to see, but I didn't expect you here."

She set the basket on the table. Megan looked inside and saw the Broken China quilt. It was the one they were working on the night little

Vernon was taken ill. Fanny took part of the quilt out and looked at Megan. She was calm but had tears in her eyes. Fanny straightened and started to talk.

"Megan, would you finish this quilt for me? I want to remember Vernon and my mother when I look at this quilt. But I just can't bring myself to finish it. All I can do is think about that night when I sit down to work on it. Those memories are too raw."

Megan placed her hand on Fanny's shoulder. "I would be honored to finish it for you. Thank you for asking."

"By the way, where *is* Liz?" Fanny asked.

Before Megan realized what she said, she blurted out, "Anna Parker is having her baby and she called for Liz to come help." Now she realized that this could be painful for Fanny and hurt her feelings. "I'm sorry, I—"

"All is good, Megan. Babies will continue to be born in our town and I will rejoice with each one. Anna helped me so much and she too has had her own heartache. Do you have any news on her progress?"

※   ※   ※

Parker wondered why it was taking so long. Was it a good sign? Trouble?

He and Samuel could hear Anna's cries and the murmurs of Liz and Mrs. Perkins reassuring and guiding her. For his wife's sake as well as for his own he earnestly prayed for a safe delivery of a healthy baby. Samuel poured another cup of coffee and encouraged him to drink it. Even Samuel had run out of conversation. Parker remembered the last baby, a boy almost to term but born alive. But the cord . . . the baby had shuddered, gasped for a breath, two breaths, then was gone. The heartache that had been Anna's was almost beyond bearing. Before that, there had been three miscarriages and one stillbirth. Still, Anna was willing to try again, hoping and praying for a healthy baby.

※   ※   ※

"No. Not yet. But I got the idea that it wouldn't be long," Megan replied.

"I will do some shopping and sit down for tea at Emma's. If you get any word, please let me know."

Megan nodded and the two grasped hands. Neither could speak.

※　※　※

Parker and Samuel looked at each other. Anna's groans had subsided. What could it mean?

"Stay with me, Anna," they heard Mrs. Perkins say firmly. "Hold my hand . . ."

Parker slumped into his chair, his heart beating wildly.

※　※　※

Barking and the sound of chickens scattering came through the back door of the mercantile as Emma burst in. She was mad as a wood rat and had a shotgun in her hand.

"That wolf pup, JoJo, is chasing my chickens again! Came straight in the henhouse even on this cold, wet day. What are Luke and Samuel going to do about it? Thomas *told* them it wouldn't work to keep that wild animal. If it gets one of my roosters . . ." Emma shuttled another round in her shotgun.

Megan and Fanny smiled at the animated Emma. "Anna is having her baby. We expect word at any time."

"Oh." Emma lowered the gun. "Let me know when you hear." She was out the back door as quickly as she came in.

"I guess JoJo got out when Samuel left to go get Mrs. Perkins this morning."

A little after lunch, Samuel came with the news that Anna and the beautiful, new baby girl were doing well. Megan, as well as the others in the mercantile, exclaimed with joy and congratulated the new uncle. The happy couple hadn't yet chosen a name, Samuel told them, guessing they wanted to be sure they would have good news this time before settling on a name and imagining the baby who would claim it. Now at last Anna held a strong, pink—"Loud!" Samuel added—bundle in her arms. Samuel's voice broke as he described the scene.

Emma found Samuel as he was leaving the mercantile. After expressing her delight about the new baby and asking all the proper questions, she told him about the wolf and her chickens. Samuel went looking for JoJo, who was growing by leaps and bounds. He needed to talk with Luke about the animal. It didn't take him long to find the silly pup, soaking wet at Emma's henhouse and looking dangerously guilty with wet feathers stuck on his paws.

"JoJo, I'm a good lawyer, but even I can't get you out of this mess." He slipped a rope around the little wolf's neck and took the wet creature, feathers and all, back to his law office. It was time to tell Luke that JoJo needed the great outdoors. He decided he would take the pup when he went south and leave him along the Crosstimber Forest. There he could hunt and maybe even join another pack. He patted the little wolf's neck and said, "Just a few more days."

Luke would have to say goodbye to his pet and let him live the life he'd been born to. Samuel hoped he was ready.

CHAPTER 18

Liz, we talked about this last time I was in town," Thomas said. "I need Luke to come to the ranch for a while. He can make up his studies, even take some with him. He needs to learn the ranch work and just plain how to work."

"He works at the store," Liz said defensively. "And he helps at home and he sweeps the floors at Emma's Table."

"Yes, I know all that, but he needs to work like a man, with other men. Emma can get one of the younger boys to help at the diner. Anyway, I hear some of the students are getting into trouble after school and I don't want Luke part of any of that. If he is out at the ranch, it will clear him of any question."

"What do you mean?" she asked and wrinkled her forehead at the comment. Luke wouldn't be involved with any trouble.

"Have you heard about the fires?"

"No. What are you talking about?"

"Have the boys been buying matches from the mercantile?"

"No," she said again. "What boys?"

"Tex said that small fires have been lit on the Perkinses' road just out of town."

"What do you mean?" she asked again trying to remember if she had heard anything about fires in the area. "I thought with the rain and cooler temperatures we've been having, fire wouldn't be a danger." She knew when there was dead ground cover, fire could be disastrous to everyone and everything. "But I haven't been here long enough to figure this weather out. It changes every fifteen minutes."

Thomas laughed. "The last rain wasn't everywhere. It was just a drizzle mostly. With our unpredictable Texas weather, fire is still an everyday concern. Whoever is starting those fires needs to be stopped and understand what they are doing."

"Who could it be?" Liz asked. "Vagrants? Squatters? Or anything to do with the conflict with Birdville?"

"No, Tex thinks some of the school kids are lighting fires on their way home and then stomping them out. He has quizzed Abby and a few students, but no luck in finding anything out. I don't want Luke here the next few weeks to be involved in any of it or know something and not be telling. Liz, it's serious, and I really need him at the ranch. Untie the apron strings or I'll have to cut them myself."

Liz didn't like what she heard about the boys starting trouble and was sure Luke wasn't involved. But on the other hand, she didn't like being bossed by Thomas either. She knew he had a point but still had her feathers ruffled by Thomas's approach. In a flash she remembered Luke's reaction when Thomas had put his foot down about the wolf pup and the sullen mood that followed. Again, she felt torn between her son and her husband.

Then she remembered her conversation with Megan about Matthew Coldwell's mother and knew she didn't want to be that way. She had so little time with Thomas as it was and didn't want to spend it fussing and being picky about the way the bone-tired man did what he needed to do. She knew he was working hard to take care of his family and plan a good life for them.

Liz took a deep breath and smiled, putting her arms around his neck. "If that's what you think is best, that's what we'll do."

Thomas was surprised but relieved. He knew he was tired and had started the conversation all wrong. He scolded himself for pushing Liz and using all the wrong words in the conversation.

"I'm sorry Liz, if I was too harsh." He bent to give her a kiss.

"I know you meant no harm and it is a good thing for Luke to go for many reasons. Tell me what he will be doing at the Rolling M."

Thomas warmed to his subject. "We are so behind with everything that needs to be done. I really should have waited to buy the herd. We need everything built and the cattle alone are a full-time job. All of the boys are working hard as they can, but winter is around the corner. Some heifers are already pregnant and we need to protect them from wolves or cougars or even coyotes." He went on to explain that the heifers would deliver in late winter or early spring, and that the calves could be lost to the elements if the weather was harsh. He explained how important managing pasture lands and water was in building up a successful ranch, how resources must be used prudently and herds well cared for.

Liz sat down and listened to Thomas share about his daily activities. It was interesting and something she didn't know much about. She wondered how Thomas had learned so much so quickly. She could tell he loved it and was a natural at it.

"Some of the calves we have now are ready to be weaned and separated from their mothers," he added.

"What do the babies think about that?"

"Oh, they bawl like you would expect but the mamas seem to be ready to separate from them. Our cook had done some laundry and had it drying on a fence. The calves came up and started sucking on the wet clothing and pulled all of the clean wash off the fence. She was as mad as she could be." Thomas misspoke and Liz caught it.

"'She'?" Her eyebrows rose. "Thomas, how can you have a young woman out there?"

Thomas recounted Bethany's story to her.

She was saddened to hear about a family abusing the young lady and was comfortable in Thomas's caretaking of her. "So the hands know?"

"Yes, and they have all vowed to treat her respectfully and keep her secret." Thomas watched Liz's reaction.

"How long will we keep her or her secret?"

"I guess as long as we need to or the Lord sees fit to change things up. The men are happy and Bet has become more relaxed. Still keeping her distance, which I think is good."

"Do you think we could somehow find Bethany's father?" Liz asked. "We could let Tex know; he might know something about the man."

Thomas chuckled over Liz wanting to fix everything. "Liz, some things just aren't fixable, but I will talk to Tex about it. Most likely, the man has gone on west or maybe he's even dead."

"It's just sad," Liz commented. "Besides the horror of what happened to Bethany, I hate it when families are torn apart and have such distance separating them." She paused. "I wish Abby and Emma could patch things up with their father too. They left on a negative note."

"Don't worry about Bethany. She is in good hands. We won't let anything bad happen to her," Thomas assured her.

"Mmm," Liz said as she thought it over.

Thomas broke into her thoughts. "The herd we got is really a great one. We have plenty of healthy females, young enough to produce many calves for years to come as long as we can supply the grass and the water. The biggest problem will be wild beasts preying on the cattle. We ride the ranch and try to eliminate the threat."

"Oh." Liz hadn't thought of that.

"Sorting the cattle, shaping the herd is our main work. Luke needs to start learning the ways of a ranch. Getting out there and doing it, making choices at the moment. Following into the sack, dead tired and getting up again when you are still wore out." After a few quiet moments Thomas asked, "How is Megan?"

"Why, what are you thinking?" Liz stopped rocking and looked at her husband.

"Jackson found me out on the ranch and asked if he could court our Miss Megan."

"Oh, what did you say?"

"I think Jackson is a fine man and that he and Megan would be a nice couple. What do you think about it?"

"Well, Megan and I have already discussed it."

Thomas stopped rocking and looked at Liz. How do women always know everything, he wondered.

"She is deciding if she would want a lawman for a husband."

"So Jackson has already made his intentions known to Megan?" Thomas asked.

"Not that I am aware of. I didn't know if Jackson was interested in Megan or not in that way, but they have a strong friendship and I wouldn't be surprised if it grew into something more."

"So what are you telling me then?" Thomas stared at his wife and couldn't get over how beautiful she was.

"Megan confided in me that she has lost her heart to Jackson and was trying to decide if she could do it or not."

Thomas just chuckled and started rocking again. "So it really is the woman that does the choosing. All these years I thought the man was in charge."

Liz laughed. "Well, if we females do a good job he thinks he is."

"So what about Abby and Samuel?" Thomas asked since Liz seemed to know it all.

"I think they could be a good match but neither is ready to accept it. I think Samuel is fighting it and Abby doesn't even know it yet. They both have a long way to go."

Thomas chuckled again. "Seems like everyone could pair up pretty quickly. How do you feel about that?"

"I want them all to be happy and have a chance at love and children. This is the way it was meant to be. Seems like Texas men are the right type for Mailly women." Liz smiled and put her hand on his as it rested on the rocker arm. "Life is a long trail when traveled alone."

After a silence, Liz began rocking again and asked, "Will you leave tomorrow?"

"No, I need one more day with you, Missy."

Liz smiled. "I'll let Luke know in the morning."

"Won't need to," Thomas replied. "He is already packed."

Once again Liz realized how much she relied on Thomas. She pulled him toward her to tell him with a kiss.

The very next day, Tex was patrolling the Perkinses' road. All day, he roamed the rolling hills and watched the grass waving in the breeze. The afternoon sun was warming his old bones as he took a break from the saddle. He was unaware that he had drifted off in his relaxed state, but screams brought him to full consciousness. He scrambled to his horse and leaped into the saddle. As he circled his horse, he saw the bellowing smoke over the rise toward the Graham place.

As he rode over the hill, he saw Georgia and Leanna huddled in the middle of the dirt road with fire leaping on both sides. The wind had pushed the flames into a dried-up thicket and beyond.

Thayer and Mr. Graham were flogging at another batch of flames with wet rags as they inched their way to the old, run-down Graham place.

Nate pumped hard on the handle of the pump as water gulped out into the trough. He plunged the bucket deep into the water and then flung it on the fire where it sizzled and blew out. He stomped at another red thread and pushed dirt at it.

Realizing the girls were safe in the dirt road, Tex went to the aid of Thayer and Mr. Graham, desperate to somehow save his shanty. Taking a shovel, he dug a dirt row, hoping the fire wouldn't jump it.

All worked in silence, now covered with sweat, dirt, and smoke. The breeze turned back and the fire stopped traveling along the thin, brown grass. Mr. Graham's run-down home was not able to elude the flames and was now falling in on itself. They all stopped to watch it tumble. Thayer and Nate looked at each other, scared and speechless, knowing that they were at fault. Nate had tear streaks down his smoky cheeks. They were too tired to run and knew it was of no use.

Tex looked at the boys. "I should horsewhip you two and drag what is left of you to your parents."

Thayer hung his head. Neither boy moved. Nate started to speak but then shut his mouth.

After several moments, Mr. Graham said, "Guess you boys did me a favor. I wanted to start things over and just didn't know how. Now you boys have helped me finally get rid of my past. Now I can build a new cabin and a new way of life for me and my boy." Mr. Graham held his head up with confidence and wiped at his face.

Tex and the boys looked at each other with confusion with this turn of events. After a moment, Tex pushed each boy forward to Mr. Graham.

"I am sorry, sir," Nate said.

Thayer glanced at Tex as he nodded his head toward the boy, encouraging him to say his piece.

"Yes," Thayer said. "We won't ever play with fire again and we will help you build up your new place. We will stop each day after school to help."

Mr. Graham nodded and looked back at the embers.

Tex told him, "You and Peter will stay with me until you're on your feet again, Graham."

Tex pulled each boy by the collar back toward the road where he gave them a good talking to. He wasn't going to let them get off that easily. When Tex had finished with the young men, he had them apologize to the little girls as well. Georgia and Leanna ran toward home. When they got to the top of the hill, they stopped to look back where Mr. Graham's shack used to stand.

Lastly, Tex took both boys home to their fathers with the news of their vandalism.

CHAPTER 19

Even though the sun was shining, Liz felt something in the air. She wasn't sure what to expect.

She stepped out the back door of the mercantile and looked at the sky. She wasn't sure which direction the weather would come from even if a storm was brewing. She circled around looking at the sky and walked to the front of the Mailly home. There was nothing except blue sky, as far as she could see. She felt cool and pulled her shawl up. The air was pleasant, but she felt a chill just the same.

She walked around to the front of the shop and looked down both directions of the main road.

"Hmm," she said and walked up the front steps to the board sidewalk in front of her store. She rubbed the back of her neck where the little hairs had stood up.

❋　❋　❋

Abby turned to see what had blown the door of her schoolroom open. She walked to the coatroom and looked around. Nothing but jackets and lunch pails lined the walls. As she stepped through the doorway, she felt a chill run across the back of her shoulders. She looked outside and decided it was only a gust of wind from the clear blue skies. She shut the door and went back to her students, dismissing any disturbance.

❋　❋　❋

Samuel had finally made it out to his ranch land and was enjoying the silence of his place. Sleeping under the stars the last few nights was exactly what he had needed. It gave him a chance to clear his mind and think. He'd been thinking too much about Abby Wilkes.

Samuel kicked his fire and poured out the almost empty coffeepot. He had ridden his land from north to south and east to west and it was a good piece of property. With his father's homestead land connecting next to it, they had quite a respectable amount of land between them. He had tried to get Anna and Pastor Parker to get the section next to theirs, but Parker had declined, explaining that he preferred to stay in town where the people needed him.

Samuel saddled his horse and decided to go see how Thomas was faring on his land, which was just next to his. With his foot on the stirrup, he mounted his horse and galloped that direction.

Pulling his horse to a stop, he looked around and thought he felt something in the air. Storm? Nothing but a fluff of a cloud floating over in the southwest. He even had his jacket in the saddlebag behind him. Over three more rises he saw Thomas just leaving his camp.

Thomas pulled his horse around and saw a rider. He didn't get much company and the first thing he thought was trouble. It had been in the air that morning when he woke. The feeling just wouldn't budge, always lingering in his thoughts like a cobweb in the corner of a room. As the rider got closer he realized it was Samuel.

"Hello, neighbor," Samuel called out when he got within the hearing distance of Thomas.

Thomas waved and kicked his horse to a gallop to meet his friend.

"How is the ranching?" Samuel asked as he pulled his horse to a stop.

"Fine, mighty fine," Thomas said and leaned across to shake Samuel's hand. "So what brings you out to the Rolling M?"

"Nothing really. I have been on my land, sleeping under the stars, just riding it, getting the lay of it," Samuel said, letting his horse nibble a little on the grass. "I was close by so thought I would ride over and see how things were going."

Thomas nodded his head letting Samuel know he was listening. "Any news from town?"

"No, no, all things just getting along normally when I left a few days ago."

"Good," Thomas said. "I had an uneasy feeling when I saw a rider, as we don't get much company out here."

"Funny you mentioned that. Something got my hackles up this morning and I brushed it off. What are you thinking?" Samuel now could feel his apprehension creeping back up. "Too late in the year for a barometer jump and tornadoes. The sky is clear blue. What do you think it is?"

"I don't know, but I think we better head for town." Thomas sprinted his pony to Bet at the chuck wagon. Samuel waited where he was, only turning his horse in the direction of Fort Worth. Thomas rode back to Samuel and they started a gallop. "Once I get a feeling like this it just gnaws at me. Let's go check it out."

※　※　※

Liz had watched at the mercantile door as she couldn't shake the feeling of unease all morning. She checked both guns and made sure one was in her apron and one under the cash drawer. She also got the rifle from the door and shuttled a new round in the chamber. At the back door, she could see all was well at the Mailly house with Megan and Emma. Nothing seemed out of place, but at the same time she knew something was, but couldn't put her finger on it. The day went along like any other.

※　※　※

"One more ridge around and we will see Fort Worth," Thomas said. Neither man had shaken off his unexplained apprehension. They looked at each other knowing they each felt compelled to get to town.

※　※　※

Abby was anxious to get the day over. Quietly her class wrote spelling words. She was banking the wood stove when the door banged open. She spun around, expecting that the wind had blown it open again.

Before her were two men she had never seen before, each holding a rifle ready for use.

She stood and spoke calmly, determined to appear composed for the sake of the children. Remembering the holdup at the mercantile, she wondered what these men could be after. She had nothing they could want. No one holds up a school for chalk. "May I help you gentlemen?"

Her students were now watching and she could see fright in their eyes. "Students, remain in your seats. These men are just lost," she said, reassuring the children.

"We want the county records," the taller man said gruffly.

Maxwell swirled in his seat and stared at his teacher. Abby silently willed him to be still and quiet. She took a step toward the boy, whose desk wasn't far from her.

"I'm not aware of the whereabouts of the papers you are requesting. Why don't you wait and let Ranger Tex or Samuel Smith, the lawyer, settle the matter for you?" Abby tried to calm the men and speak reason to them.

"No! No! They are ours!" one man burst out.

"They are in cahoots with Fort Worth anyway," the other growled. "We came to get what is ours."

※　※　※

At the mercantile, Liz's misgivings had grown. She bid her departing customer goodbye and went to the front door. Looking down both directions of the main road, she noticed two unfamiliar horses at the school. What could they be doing there? Whose were they?

Ever mindful of the holdup that had resulted in her grandfather's death, she had resolved never to be caught unprepared again. She picked up the rifle she kept behind her counter, closed and locked her store, and headed toward the school.

※　※　※

One man walked up the row between the desk and pulled Georgia from her chair.

"Teacher, I want those papers. Now get them!"

Maxwell started to get up and the man pushed him back down in his chair. "Mister, I—"

"Maxwell," Abby warned him, "just be still. This is a grownup matter."

Georgia squirmed against his hold.

"Please, sir, we don't have what you came looking for. This is a classroom and you're frightening the children." Abby silently prayed that the situation would not get out of hand and that the men would leave peaceably. "Let that child go immediately."

"Sit down, teacher, if you don't want trouble."

Abby gladly moved to her desk, knowing she had a gun tucked in one drawer. If only she could find the courage to use it if need be. Georgia whimpered as the stranger pulled her up tight.

"Lady, I'm only gonna ask one more time!"

The man in the back started to move up the aisle to Abby's desk.

Nate and Thayer eyed each other, as he passed the back row where they were. They each put a foot out, tripping him, so he fell flat on his face. As he struggled to regain his footing, his rifle went off. Children screamed and ducked under their desks. Nate and Thayer tackled him, and Leon, clutching at his upper arm, charged after his accomplice, knocking him over with a head butt.

Abby grabbed Georgia from him and pushed her under her own desk.

✕　✕　✕

Liz started running as soon as she heard the shot. Just as she was about to climb the steps she saw Thomas and Samuel pull their horses to a stop. Thomas motioned for her to stand aside as he and Samuel darted inside. Liz scampered in behind them.

Abby drew a sigh of relief as she saw her cavalry arrive in the nick of time.

"What's going on here?" Samuel asked, eyes darting over the room. He took in the situation immediately, and he and Thomas quickly dispatched the two gunmen, tying them up with ropes and gagging their mouths for good measure. They sent word for the Rangers to come and transport them to the Birdville jail.

Thomas clapped the boys on the back and congratulated them for their bravery. He suspected Luke would be disappointed that he had been out at the ranch and missed the excitement and reflected that having a son to be proud of was a desirable thing. Or a daughter. As he looked around, he saw that the schoolgirls, who came from sturdy stock, would recover well from the ordeal.

"What did they want?" Samuel asked Abby.

"The county papers, those dreadful county records."

"What's this?" Liz asked. "Blood?"

Leon's arm had been grazed by the errant bullet from the rifle, but it turned out to be a very minor wound. Liz and Abby cleaned and wrapped it, and instructed him to be sure his parents kept it clean. She could tell the boy was proud of his slight injury. What a story he would have to tell! Liz shook her head at all the DeJarnette family had gone through in the past weeks.

After the excitement had died down, Maxwell looked up at his teacher. "Miss Wilkes, did you lie to the bad men?"

Abby blinked and took a breath. "I hope not. I'm not sure." She paused. "I do not have the papers, nor are they in this classroom."

Maxwell smiled and nodded his head, reassuring his teacher that he understood.

Chapter 20

Christmas was finally just a few days away. Abby's students had been practicing for the Christmas pageant and were doing a superb job on their roles. The lines had all been committed to memory and everyone knew their cues.

The weather had been unusually cold during the month but today the sun was out and it was just brisk. Samuel lit the stove early at the school and the room already had the chill knocked off. He had surprised Abby often with that task. She would thank Samuel as soon as she saw him.

Her students were finishing up with their spelling words, easy ones at the top, harder ones at the bottom as usual. Each student worked as far down the board as possible. Each day they showed improvement in their abilities, but today they were restless with the excitement in the air.

Maxwell came to *Santa Claus* and piped up, "Teacher, do you believe in Santa Claus?"

Abby looked up, unprepared for the question. "They tell me if you don't believe, he won't come," Abby answered.

Leanna and Georgia had an innocent sparkle in their eye as they thought of the jolly old elf with toys in his pack.

Lillie and her sister Daisy sat together on the bench. Lillie popped her head up to ask a question. "Do reindeers really fly?"

Abby nearly said automatically, "No *s* on reindeer; one reindeer, two reindeer," but realized that lesson time was over and the magic of the holiday excitement was just too strong to continue with any schoolwork. So she only said again, "That's what they tell me."

Then she directed an inquiry to the four oldest boys in her class. "Luke, Nate, Thayer, Leon. Did you bring your gloves today?" Luke had returned for the last week of the term before Christmas.

"Yes, ma'am," they chanted.

"Good. Would you like to go out into the woods behind the school and find a nice Christmas tree for the church and school?"

"Yes, ma'am!"

"Good," she repeated. "Look for a straight one about this tall." Abby stood and held her hand just a little above her head. "Be careful and be back at lunch or just a little later."

The boys were already bundling up in jackets, hats, and gloves. Nate and Thayer were proud to be trusted with the task. Their horses were tethered outside where they stomped their hooves, shook their manes, and nickered at their masters. They wanted to run in the brisk sunshine too.

As the door shut, Daisy turned to Miss Wilkes. "Do we get to make ornaments for the tree?"

"Yes, I have plans for popcorn roping, white paper snowflakes, berries here in this basket for stringing, and Christmas cards for your parents."

The students were in a big buzz as they looked at each other with delight and anticipation.

"This is the best day ever," Daisy cried excitedly. The students worked together and sang Christmas carols as they rejoiced in the Christmas season.

Not a single one asked if it was lunchtime and they continued to work on their decorations right through it. Maxwell stopped and said, "Listen. Do you hear that?" He paused. "The boys are back with the tree!"

Everyone jumped up and looked out the window. They could see the boys dragging a big tree behind them with a rope. The gang was singing at the top of their lungs, "O Christmas Tree, O Christmas Tree . . ."

Abby looked over the heads of her younger pupils and saw the boys coming toward the school. She was proud of her class and the progress they made in all areas of their lives. The young men dragging the tree would only be in her classroom a little longer and then they would soon grow up to be men ready to tackle the world. She smiled as she thought of the leadership they would bring to Fort Worth. They were all handsome, smart, and talented.

Little Dove was new to most of the holiday tradition. "Do we bring it inside?"

"Yes," Lillie said and giggled. "We even put candles on it. Well, sometimes," Daisy added. Everyone knew about what happened to the Graham place. There would be no candles on an indoor tree this year.

The boys brought the tree inside, trimmed a few unruly branches, and nailed boards to the bottom so it would stand.

Daisy and Nate placed the berry roping along the top while Thayer and Leon added some popcorn strings to the bottom. Luke was working on a star cut from a tin can that would hold a paper candle and be put at the very top. The younger students hooked the paper snowflakes to the branches until the tree was completely covered. They stood back to admire their handiwork proudly.

"Just wait till Papa sees it." Daisy was a daddy's girl at heart and everyone knew it.

"Yes, it is lovely, just lovely," Abby praised. "Let's double-check our costumes for the play tomorrow and then we will dismiss early today."

"My stomach's talking," Maxwell said as he rubbed his belly. "We worked right through our lunchtime and I didn't even notice."

It was a first for Maxwell.

※　※　※

The next morning, Tex slipped through the back door of Emma's Table. "Do you have it ready?" he asked.

"Yes, do you want to put it on and see that it fits?"

Emma and Megan were all smiles as the red suit was held up before him. Megan had even made a long white beard from sheep's wool. Tex stood behind a curtain in his red long johns and stepped into the Santa suit. He had let his curly gray hair grow and started a beard back when the cold weather kicked in.

When he stepped out from around the curtain Megan's hands flew up to her mouth. "Oh my, Tex. You do look like ole Saint Nick himself." She fussed with the wool beard, working it into his real beard and curly locks.

"If I didn't believe before, I certainly would now." Emma stood and stared at the image of Santa Claus before her.

Tex placed a hand on his wide black belt. "Ho, ho, ho," he sang out and laughed at himself. Emma and Megan joined in with him.

The school Christmas pageant was to start late in the afternoon with a Christmas meal afterward and would include all the families. The students would then have a gift exchange of something that they had made. Abby had them draw names several weeks before and expected them to not tell whose name they had gotten. Even Maxwell did a good job with keeping the secret of the name he drew.

The air was plentiful with excitement as wagonloads of families started to arrive in town. The sky was gray and Jackson predicted snow was coming.

The students gathered in the school as their families visited on the side of the church. Everyone was in town. The Coopers visited with the Wiltons and the Turners. Georgia's mother laughed with Mrs. Wheeler over the story of Vera June under the school, while they stood close to the warmth of the stove. Over by the tree, the Tates and DeJarnettes talked about the election of President Buchanan and how weak they predicted he would be. They all agreed that they would not have been happy with any of the three choices. Even Chet, John, and Blue stayed in town for the celebration. Liz's freight line was on holiday through the New Year. It was good to spend time with old friends.

The church and school were about to burst at the seams when Ranger Jackson and Colt stepped inside. "Look. It's snowing," Jackson bragged as he shook snowflakes from his jacket.

Colt slapped him on the back. "Yeah, Jackson always has to be right. We rode in from up north and drug it back with us."

The group chuckled and looked at the unusual weather as the fluffy flakes floated down. The snow danced and swirled outside the window, stacking up on the wagon seats and the backs of the horses.

"Where is Tex?" Abby asked as she looked around the crowded room.

"He's around, will be back any moment," Jackson answered. Liz and Thomas were the last to enter with Buck and Clyde.

They scooted past Anna and Pastor Parker who were drinking cider with Smithy and Samuel. Parker held his newborn daughter. He cradled the sleeping beauty in a pink crocheted blanket, all lacy around the edges.

Tex slipped in the back door with Zeke Goodwin and old man Jeb. Even Mr. Graham showed up with a shaved face and combed hair.

Jeremiah and Katie Longmont were the first to sit down on the church pews. Katie cradled the bottom of her tight stomach as she scooted down the bench and made room for Anna. The new mother proudly sat in the front row with Katie and swaddled her baby girl in white cloth. Anna's little Hope Rose would play the baby Jesus in the program. The students quietly laughed and whispered as they bumped into angel wings and the gift of myrrh that Nate held. He was one of the three kings.

Abby went back to her students. "Are you ready to start?" she asked the gleaming faces before her. Each child in the school was costumed to participate in the program, though not all had speaking parts.

Emma and Megan signaled Abby that all was ready for the play to begin. The teacher clapped her hands, welcomed the guests, and the program began.

Luke took his place as the narrator off to one side of the stage. Liz couldn't help noting how handsome he looked and wondered if this year would be his last as a student in a school pageant. "Mary and Joseph traveled far from Galilee to Bethlehem," he announced in his newly deepening voice, setting the scene.

Peter and Little Dove, as Joseph and Mary, came to the center of the stage. Tiny Hope Rose slept in her big sister Little Dove's arms, unaware she had been cast as baby Jesus.

Luke narrated the story. "While they were in Bethlehem, Mary gave birth to her firstborn son, and wrapped him in swaddling clothes, and laid him in a manger because there was no room for them in the inn."

Georgia and Maxwell were dressed as shepherds and walked to the center. Maxwell giggled and Georgia elbowed him to get serious. Georgia carried her fat white milk-puppy, Penny Ann, with handmade lamb ears tied to her head. Vera June was close by, also playing a sheep.

Luke went on, "And there were in the same country shepherds abiding in the field, keeping watch over their flock by night. And lo, the angel of the Lord came upon them, and the glory of the Lord shone round about them; and they were sore afraid."

Georgia and Maxwell pretended to shake in fright as Daisy appeared as an angel. Maxwell was so dramatic some in the audience tittered with appreciation. Daisy's angel wings were made of chicken feathers that Emma had been saving.

"And the angel said unto them:"

"Fear not; for behold, I bring you good tidings of great joy, which shall be to all people. For unto you is born this day in the city of David a Saviour, which is Christ the Lord." Daisy stood proudly with her angel wings spread wide. She had remembered every word perfectly.

"And suddenly there was with the angel a multitude of the heavenly host praising God and saying—" Luke's voice was authoritative as he quoted the Bible passage from memory.

Lillie and Leanna, with their own angel wings made from chicken feathers, came to stand by Daisy and continued the story. "Glory to God in the highest and on earth peace, good will toward men." Their little voices tried to be strong as they proclaimed the good news of Jesus' birth.

"Later, wise men from Eastern lands found Jesus, the newborn King, in Bethlehem." Luke continued the story.

Nate, Thayer, and Leon strode regally in their kingly robes—donated from someone's storage chest—as three wise men. They sported colorful turbans designed by Megan around their heads and carried wrapped gifts. Nate stepped forward. "Where is he that is born King of the Jews?"

"We have seen his star in the east," Thayer voiced.

"We are come to worship him." Leon bowed as he gave his lines. His parents, grateful for restored health and all the blessings of the season, had shining eyes as they watched their son.

When the story part of the pageant ended, the students stood together and sang some familiar Christmas songs.

As the sweet strains of the music faded, the door suddenly burst open and snowflakes swirled in around the jolly elf. "Santa Claus!" the younger children mouthed with bright eyes and wondering faces. The night was white behind him as the snow was piling up, covering everything.

"Ho, ho, ho," Tex bellowed, thoroughly relishing his role as St. Nick.

Jackson and Colt took a double take until they recognized Tex.

He ambled down the center aisle of the church spreading good cheer. He had an old burlap sack over his shoulder, filled with surprises. He reached into the bag and found a peppermint stick or an apple for each person. Also in the bag were gifts for Abby's students—hand-carved horses for the younger boys and doll dresses for the girls. The older boys were given pocketknives.

The children held their gifts close to their hearts and looked at Santa with wonder. Daisy and Little Dove each received a heart-shaped charm. Daisy kissed Santa on the cheek as he bent down to hand it to her. "Merry Christmas!" Tex called out as he exited the side door of the church.

Maxwell yelled out, "Santa!" Tex stopped and turned to the little boy clutching his hand-carved horse and candy. "I love you!"

Tex was very pleased. "Merry Christmas, son. Merry Christmas."

The room was silent with the door ajar and snow twirling in around the red suit as it disappeared into the night. Sleigh bells were heard and

Maxwell ran to the door and pushed it open.

"I believe, Santa, I believe," Maxwell whispered into the empty, crisp darkness.

Whispers and voices asked, "Who was that?"

Maxwell piped up again. "Santa. That was Santa Claus."

It wasn't long before the meal was ready and placed on the big long tables. Families and friends visited and ate throughout the school and church. It was a happy, merry time as the community celebrated peace and goodwill.

Abby finished passing out her own gifts to the students. She had made hand-embroidered hankies with their initials on the corner.

Tex changed from his Santa suit and slipped back into the group unnoticed.

Megan searched for Fanny Wilton and handed Fanny's basket back to her with the finished Broken China quilt. Fanny hugged her tightly in thanks.

Jackson had nailed some mistletoe to the top of the archway between the church and school. He pulled Megan over and kissed her on the cheek. "Merry Christmas, Megan."

She returned with a hug. "Merry Christmas, Jackson," she whispered.

"Come watch this," Jackson said as he held her hand and led her over to where Colt and Tex were sitting by the fire. Colt placed a squirming bag on Tex's lap. A fat little puppy with a black nose jumped out and licked Tex.

"Merry Christmas, boss," Jackson said. "To replace your old dog, Annie," Colt added. "She will be real good. I'll help you train her."

Tex was speechless. Life could give back to a weathered old man who had made his share of mistakes. He had asked the Lord for ways to give to others, and now he had been blessed in return.

The door creaked open again and their old friend, the peddler Skelly, appeared. "Is there any room in the inn?" His belly shook as he laughed at his own joke.

Megan and Emma ushered him to the warmth and showed him the

food table. He smiled with anticipation as he viewed the feast. Colt was close behind.

Samuel and Abby found themselves pushed together by the crowd when Samuel looked up and noticed they were just below the sprig of mistletoe. He put his arm around Abby's waist and gently pulled her toward him for a Christmas kiss. "Merry Christmas, teacher."

Abby smiled and closed her eyes.

Thomas didn't need mistletoe as an excuse to give Liz a long kiss. When he pulled back he said, "I love you. Merry Christmas."

Liz smiled up to her husband and whispered, "Merry Christmas —Papa!"

"What?"

"We're going to have a baby." She laughed at his stunned face.

Thomas shook off his bewilderment and replied with a smile spread across his face. "I think that is the best news second to the Christmas story!"

Liz thought about the past few months and all that they had held. She looked around the room at the friends and family and realized they were each a thread that made this new place home. Her heart was filled with joy and contentment. She leaned into Thomas and reflected, God is good; He is very, very good.

A Word of Thanks

I want to thank God from whom all blessings flow. God had a plan for my life and He has a plan for yours. He states it over and over again in the book of Ephesians. When Jesus Christ walked the earth, He showed us how to live that life. Then the Holy Spirit helps you as you walk it out each day. He continues to pour out His promises and fulfill His Scripture. Thank You, Jesus. I'm so very grateful for Your storehouse of blessings!

ACKNOWLEDGMENTS

Thank you to my best friend and husband, Steve. You taught me how to dream and have always been supportive of my endeavors. I love you.

My two wonderful sons, Nick and Tucker: You both were always there to give ideas, tote a box, drive a truck, or set up a trade show booth. Thank you for your love and advice. To Nick's wife Amber: the daughter-in-law I prayed for, before you were even born. You are a great addition to our family, a wonderful wife and mother to our precious granddaughter, Lydia. You all bless my heart.

To my mother and many sisters, plus my niece Briley: Thank you for keeping life fun and always giving me more story lines for the next book. You are breath to me, sweet ladies!

Jenny, my assistant, and to Elaine as well: Thank you for all of your hard work and effort. You keep my life in order for all of those many time slots I have. You are sweet friends and I love you.

Thank you, Moody Publishers, for bringing my women to life.

About the Author

Jodi Barrows is an author, speaker, and quilting revolutionary. She speaks to quilting audiences throughout the United States and around the world, weaving in the story of the Mailly cousins as she goes. Her unique teaching method includes her Square in a Square quilting technique. Jodi has produced dozens of teaching tools and developed several fabric lines. Commissioned to compose quilts for state and national organizations, Jodi also worked with the Kansas Historical Society. She enjoys spending time with her family and her husband, Steve, her high school sweetheart. For more about Jodi, her novels, and the Square in a Square method of quilting, go to her website at: www.squareinasquare.com.

TAKE THE LIFE-CHANGING JOURNEY WITH

A BELOVED FAMILY WHO EXPERIENCES

HEARTACHE, NEW BEGINNINGS, ADVENTURE,

AND THE BEAUTIFUL QUILTS THAT

BIND THEM TOGETHER.

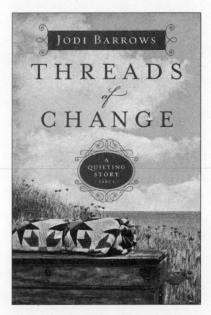

9-780-8024-0937-9

In 1856, Lucas Mailly gathers his granddaughters and sends them west. With every turn along the wagon trail, these cousins, filled with city social graces, charm, and love for quilting, must master the frontier to become true warriors of their hearts, minds, and souls.

Also available as an ebook

IMPACTING LIVES THROUGH THE POWER OF STORY

www.RiverNorthFiction.com | www.MoodyPublishers.com

Renew your Hope in the Power of the Unexpected

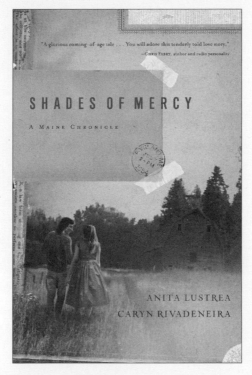

It's 1954 and the far Northwoods of Maine are about to change. Mercy Millar is ready for the world to embrace her as the young woman she is—as well as embrace the forbidden love she feels for Mick, a Maliseet boy who works on her father's farm. When racial tensions escalate and Mick is thrown in jail under suspicion of murder, Mercy nearly loses all hope—in love, in her father, and in God himself.

Also available as an ebook

river north

IMPACTING LIVES THROUGH THE POWER OF STORY

www.RiverNorthFiction.com | www.MoodyPublishers.com

IMPACTING LIVES THROUGH THE POWER OF STORY

Thank you! We are honored that you took the time out of your busy schedule to read this book. If you enjoyed what you read, would you consider sharing the message with others?

- Write a review online at amazon.com, bn.com, goodreads.com, cbd.com.

- Recommend this book to friends in your book club, workplace, church, school, classes or small group.

- Go to facebook.com/RiverNorthFiction, "like" the page and post a comment as to what you enjoyed the most.

- Mention this book in a Facebook post, Twitter update, Pinterest pin or a blog post.

- Pick up a copy for someone you know who would be encouraged by this message.

- Subscribe to our newsletter for information on upcoming titles, inside information on discounts and promotions, and learn more about your favorite authors at RiverNorthFiction.com.